D0182298

Jinx

Chocolate Wishes

'A deliciously enchanting
modern-day fairy tale'
Books Etc

'Witty and wicked, a brill read'
Mizz

'Devour the magic – hilarious
and absorbing'
Irish Independent

About the author

Fiona Dunbar began her career as an illustrator of children's books, as well as writing three picture books. But it was reading to her own children that inspired her to write her first novel, *The Truth Cookie*, closely followed by *Cupid Cakes* and *Chocolate Wishes* – which together make the hugely popular Lulu Baker trilogy (now filmed as Jinx for CBBC!). Since then Fiona has also written *Toonhead*, and the exciting Silk Sisters trilogy: *Pink Chameleon*, *Blue Gene Baby* and *Tiger-lily Gold*.

Fiona loves cooking almost as much as storytelling. With both, she tends to make things up as she goes along, and the result can sometimes be surprising! She lives in London with her husband and two children.

Jinx

Chocolate Wishes

fiona dunbar

ORCHARD BOOKS

Thanks to my lovely policeman cousin Mat, for his patient
indulgence and helpful insights. Thanks also to Ann-Janine
for her incredible instinct, and to Margaret Clark for being so
encouraging. And thanks to Catherine Coe, for taking it all in
her stride! Last, but not least, thanks to my daughter Helena
for her help on all three Lulu books – and for laughing in all
the right places!

ORCHARD BOOKS
338 Euston Road
London NW1 3BH
Orchard Books Australia
Hachette Children's Books Australia
Level 17/207 Kent Street, Sydney, NSW 2000

ISBN 978 1 40830 746 5

First published in Great Britain in 2005
This TV tie-in edition first published in 2009

A paperback original

Text © Fiona Dunbar 2005

1 3 5 7 9 10 8 6 4 2

Printed in Great Britain

Orchard Books is a division of Hachette Children's Books,
an Hachette UK company
www.hachette.co.uk

For Celia, the Charlottes, Danni, Emerald, Kara, Leah, Rachael, Rosalind, Saskia, Shirlene, Caroline & Victoria, and Yasmin…and all the other erstwhile year 6's we miss so much!

Contents

Cut an apple in half across its width. There, in each half, you will see a five-pointed star. Two stars: one represents Venus, the evening star, also known as Hesperus; the other is your star, the one which speaks to you, and only you, across time and space. Now imagine a magnificent garden surrounded by waters. It shares its name with Hesperus, which shines above it. In this garden are three nymphs, who guard a tree which bears golden apples. Very few people ever reach into that world and learn its secrets. You are one of them.

The first secret is this: anything and everything is possible.

The rest of the secrets that have been entrusted to me, I share with you in the following pages. Let your star guide you in using them.

From the introduction to *The Apple Star*, by Ambrosia May

Finding Roots

To begin with, there had been just one small secret, but as is the way with such things, that secret grew up, got married and started having babies. Before she knew it, Lulu Baker had lots of secrets, and the only person she allowed herself to share them with was Amanda Fry – or Frenchy to her friends, after 'French Fry'. Frenchy had been in on the whole magic recipe book business right from the start, including this new development: the growing of ingredients in Lulu's own back garden. Frenchy had seen the note Lulu had received from Cassandra, her mentor and supplier of magical ingredients, on midsummer night:

Dear Lulu,

Congratulations! You have successfully carried out three recipes (although recipe no. 2 did not have the desired effect, it was nevertheless done with good intent and had

A HAPPY OUTCOME). YOUR SUCCESS HAS BEEN DUE TO THE CONVICTION YOU HAVE DEMONSTRATED, AND THE TALENT YOU HAVE SHOWN IN CREATIVE COOKING AND NURTURING YOUR PLANTS. THEREFORE, YOU QUALIFY TO MOVE UP TO THE NEXT GRADE OF RESPONSIBILITY, WHICH IS TO BUILD YOUR OWN PRIVATE STORE OF INGREDIENTS — IF YOU WISH TO DO SO. YOUR INHERITANCE OF THE APPLE STAR IS A LEGACY YOU SHOULD CONTINUE, AND THIS IS THE NEXT STEP IN THAT PROCESS. I VERY MUCH HOPE YOU WILL, AND ENCLOSE THESE SEEDS AS A GESTURE OF MY FAITH IN YOU. PLEASE PLANT THEM, AND WE WILL SPEAK AGAIN VERY SOON.

LOVE,

CASSANDRA

Excited, Lulu had planted those seeds – for something called the Creeping Crillow – the very next day. However she found lately that Dad had been asking rather too many questions about her unusual plants. But she could hardly blame him; they really were *very* unusual...

*

Lulu pressed the latest batch of seeds into the moist ground, covered them with earth and patted it down. A fine rain filled the garden with the musty dead-leaf smell of autumn. Lulu liked this smell; with it would come the spiced-wine smell of Halloween parties, and the toffee apple and burnt-out firework smell of Guy Fawkes Night.

The tinkle of wind chimes mingled with soft, whispering voices. Ignoring the voices, Lulu sat back on her heels and wiped her hands on her gardening trousers. 'There! That's the last planting of the season,' she told Frenchy.

'What kind of plant is it?' asked Frenchy, eagerly.

'It's a Zizyphus shrub,' said Lulu. 'Like that one over there.' She nodded towards a small bush with ripe red fruits. 'The fruit's really yummy – but don't taste one, it'll make you zonk out. It goes into something called the Sandman Smoothie; sends you to sleep instantly. I always make sure I have it at bedtime!'

There were those whispering voices again.

Hearing them, Frenchy peered in the direction they were coming from and frowned. The voices stopped. Frenchy shrugged and gazed around. 'Place looks amazing, Lu,' she remarked, casting her eye over the vivid jungle Lulu had created. 'So which one's the Creeping Crillow, then?'

'That one over there,' said Lulu, pointing to a rather unremarkable plant with feathery leaves and little blue flowers.

'That's it?' said Frenchy. 'It looks so...ordinary.'

'Just wait till you see it in action!' said Lulu. The Creeping Crillow got its name because it was so averse to direct sunlight, it would actually cross the garden to avoid it. Lulu peered up at the pale grey sky. 'Mind you, it's kind of dull right now, so don't know if it'll do anything.' As she spoke, the whispering voices grew louder. Lulu turned around to face the small tree with pretty drooping branches that stood behind her. 'Sh!' she hissed, and the tree immediately fell silent.

Frenchy giggled. 'I take it that's the Idzumo tree!'

Lulu rolled her eyes, but couldn't help grinning slightly. 'Yeah, that's right. Honestly, it starts muttering away whenever you're talking near it, like it's trying to join in the conversation. There it goes again! – *shush*, will you!' Lulu linked arms with Frenchy and guided her to the other side of the garden. She had learnt of this chattering tree the first time she had met Cassandra; Idzumo honey had been a vital ingredient in the Truth Cookies Lulu had made, which compelled the eater to tell the truth about everything. The idea of a talking tree was just too irresistible to Lulu, and after some persuasion

Cassandra had finally agreed to let her have a young sapling.

'Well, Cassandra did warn you it could be annoying,' Frenchy reminded her.

'Yeah, I know. I just really wanted it!' Lulu admitted. 'Hey, check this one out,' she added, leading Frenchy over to a low, spreading plant with large white trumpet-like flowers. At the base of each flower grew little squash that resembled yellow cucumbers. Sushi, the neighbour's cat, wandered close to the plant and sniffed. All of a sudden, the plant squirted a clear fluid from the centre of its flower, right into the cat's face.

Miaoow! screeched Sushi, as she dashed back over the fence to the tranquil calm of her own garden.

Lulu giggled. 'Now you know why it's called the Squirting Squash.'

'Oh, that's the one you used in—'

'The Upside-Down Cake, that's right,' said Lulu. 'Brilliant, eh?' The juice from the Squirting Squash – a challenge to collect – had been a prime ingredient in this cake, which had become a regular favourite of Lulu's. The Upside-Down Cake was for lightening the mood of excessively serious people, and Lulu had found it worked wonders on some of the teachers at school. Lessons had never been so much fun.

'Ah, there you are, Noodle,' said Lulu's dad as he emerged from the back door. 'Hi, Frenchy.'

'Oh! Uh, hello,' said Frenchy, a little taken aback at first. Although Lulu had told her how Dad's hair had changed, it was the first time she'd seen it. He *did* look very different.

Lulu's dad smiled and ran his fingers through his hair. 'How are your mum and dad?' he asked.

'Oh, brilliant, thank you!' said Frenchy.

'You have a nice holiday?'

Frenchy looked flushed with happiness. 'Yes, thanks. It was...lovely to go together.' That had been Lulu's big success with the Cupid Cakes – bringing Frenchy's parents, Jack and Jill, back together.

'I'm sure,' said Lulu's dad. Lulu couldn't help noticing a wistful look in his eye; it was now nine years since Mum had died. Lulu had been so little, she had no memory of holidays with the three of them; all she had were the pictures.

Dad gazed skywards. 'Ah, brightening up at last, I see!'

Lulu hadn't noticed, but indeed a patch of blue had appeared, pouring the early October sun's rays directly on the Creeping Crillow. She and Frenchy exchanged nervous glances; Dad had yet to witness the Crillow mid-creep. In fact he hadn't even noticed that this modest-looking plant appeared in different flower beds at various times of the day.

Lulu's dad smoothed his hair back again. 'Well, give your parents my best, won't you?' he told Frenchy on his way back indoors. 'We must get together soon.'

'I will, thank you,' said Frenchy.

Immediately Dad's back was turned, Lulu and Frenchy swivelled in unison, eyeing the Creeping Crillow in anticipation. Sure enough, the sun had begun to bother it, so it pulled its chunky, stout-legged roots out of the ground and began to stroll over to the shady side of the garden. It did so without making the slightest sound, yet Dad suddenly turned back.

'Oh by the way, I was going to make some—' He stopped abruptly and stared. The three of them stood, marvelling at the plant as it walked over to a nice shady spot and silently slid its roots back into the soft ground. It wiggled its bottom as it lowered itself into place, then spread out its stems contentedly. Lulu couldn't help letting out a nervous giggle, and this set Frenchy off too.

Dad rubbed his eyes. 'Did that really just happen?'

'Um...' said Lulu, before bursting into laughter again.

Dad cleared his throat. 'Look, Lulu, you know I told you about that college friend of mine who became a botanist—'

'No, Dad, *please*,' insisted Lulu, tugging on his sleeve. She paused; mustn't sound too desperate, she thought. But if Dad's botanist friend were told about her plants, then the next thing she knew, everything about her magical recipe book, *The Apple Star*, and what Lulu had done with the Truth Cookies and the Cupid Cakes would be out in the open. 'It's just that – well...' she trailed off, unable to come up with a plausible excuse.

'Oh, don't be so silly Noodle! It's just fascinating, that's all. What harm could possibly—'

'Ahem,' interrupted Frenchy, adjusting her glasses. 'Lulu, I guess we'll have to let your dad in on our little secret.'

Lulu gaped at her in disbelief. Surely she wouldn't!

'See, the thing is,' said Frenchy to Lulu's dad, 'you know how *my mum* is really into growing veggies and stuff?' She glanced briefly at Lulu as she said the words 'my mum', to quell her alarm.

'Yes?'

'Well...how do I put this? Some of the species she grows are imported and, well, she brought them over herself, you see. Which, uh, isn't strictly legal. When Lulu got into the gardening thing too, Mum let her have some seeds and cuttings. So we really would rather you didn't, you know, tell anyone. If that's OK...?'

Good old Frenchy, thought Lulu, heaving a sigh of relief. What a clever idea; Frenchy was a quick thinker.

Dad frowned and shook his head.

'*Please*, Dad?' said Lulu, still clinging to his arm and treating him to the most soulful doe-eyed look she could muster. 'We don't want to get Jill into trouble, do we?'

Dad ran his fingers through his hair and sighed. 'Look, it's not that I want to get anyone into trouble, it's just...for heaven's sake, a plant just walked across my garden!'

'Sh!' hissed Lulu. 'You want the neighbours to hear?'

'*Sh! Pss haha wissy babble gradilibam!*' went the Idzumo tree.

Dad sighed heavily and shook his head again. 'Oh, good grief!' he said. 'I'm going for a walk...' He turned and headed off through the side gate.

Fizzy Strawberry Sherbet

'Hey, girls!' said Aileen. She was wearing two coats and three hats all at once, and carried a sheepskin rug, a boom box, an oriental parasol, a shop-window mannequin with blue eyelashes, and a long, wooden object that was taller than herself. Aileen, the Australian housekeeper, normally lived out. But she had just found herself without a place to live after a problem with a devious landlord, so Lulu's dad had offered to put her up for a few weeks, until she found another flat.

Having no other immediate family besides Dad, Lulu found the prospect of Aileen actually living with them – even for a short time – quite absurdly thrilling. She chuckled at the sight of Aileen, and particularly the mannequin. 'Hey, you brought me a dolly, excellent!'

'That's actually her name,' laughed Aileen. 'Say hello, Dolly!'

'Hello, Dolly,' said Dad, smoothing his hair back as he appeared beside Lulu and Frenchy. Lulu was glad to see his mood had lifted since he had gone off in a huff earlier on. 'Here, let me help you. Where's the rest of the stuff?' He reached out to relieve Aileen of some of her things.

'Thanks, Michael. There's just the backpack and a suitcase in the car...ooh, careful with me didgeridoo – don't want to scratch the walls!' she said, as Dad grappled with the huge wooden instrument.

Lulu and Frenchy took the parasol and the boom box. 'Hey, we can have a disco party in your room!' suggested Lulu as they headed up the stairs.

'Lulu!' said Dad, his hair flopping in front of his face as he lumbered up the stairs with the mannequin and the didgeridoo. 'Give Aileen a chance to settle in, love!'

'Oh, that's all right, Michael!' said Aileen. 'I don't mind having the girls hang out with me for a while. Hey, I think Dolly's taken a shine to you!'

'That's what...she tells all the guys,' quipped Dad, breathlessly.

'I know – steals all my blokes,' laughed Aileen. 'Wish I had a figure like that!'

Lulu laughed too, but couldn't help being reminded of Aileen's most recent break-up, with Phil the drummer. None of Aileen's boyfriends ever seemed to last more than six months, which in Phil's case was probably just as well; he had been as dull as a wet Tuesday evening in March. All those failed relationships had to make Aileen fed up, Lulu thought, yet nothing ever seemed to get her down; in the three years Lulu had known her, Aileen had always been this bright, fizzy strawberry sherbet of a person.

Once everything was assembled in her room, Aileen began removing her coats. 'Here, catch!' she said, throwing Lulu and Frenchy some sweets she'd found in her pocket.

Lulu caught one and jumped on the bed. 'Hey, we can have midnight feasts – that'd be fun, wouldn't it?'

'Where I come from, we used to have midnight barbies on the beach!' laughed Aileen, opening her suitcase. 'Too bloomin' cold for that here!'

'Sounds brilliant,' said Frenchy. 'Why'd you want to leave?'

'Oh London's really ace…and where would I be without my Lulu, eh?' She ruffled Lulu's hair.

Lulu sucked on her sweet. 'Ooh, it's going to be *so* much nicer with you in this room than when the dreaded Torquil was staying here.'

Aileen grimaced. 'Ugh! Wonder what sort of horrors he's up to now.' Torquil was the son of

Varaminta le Bone, who just over a year ago had almost succeeded in dragging Lulu's dad up the aisle. Almost. But Lulu's Truth Cookie recipe had averted that particular disaster...

'Basking in fame and fortune, no doubt, now his mum's a telly star,' said Frenchy. 'I saw that programme the other night.'

'Ooh, sh!' hissed Lulu. 'We don't mention That Show in this house! Not while Dad's around, anyway.'

Varaminta's career had taken an interesting turn lately. She had been much in demand many years ago as a fashion model, but things had gone rapidly downhill thereafter. She had been trying to claw her way back up to stardom ever since, but her attempts had been increasingly desperate – until she was invited to star in the TV makeover show, *The Fashion Police*. The 'Fashion Police' consisted of Varaminta and two accomplices, whose mission was to barge unannounced into the homes of ordinary folk and remodel their victims' entire lifestyles...and 'victims' they certainly were; Varaminta was merciless.

'Don't think I could stomach watching it anyway,' said Aileen, putting some clothes in a drawer.

'She was particularly horrible to you, wasn't she?' said Frenchy.

'I'll say she was!' Lulu chipped in. 'Giving her the

sack like that for no reason...except of course that Aileen *saw right through* her – didn't you, Aileen?'

'Well, let's just say I wasn't sure she was, *ahem*, right for your dad...'

'Yeah, I bet she was jealous of you too, because you're pretty,' added Lulu.

'Oh! Remember the ghastly Grodmila?' said Frenchy. Grodmila was the grim barrel-shaped Grizlonian Varaminta had replaced Aileen with.

'"I vont to clean here now",' said Lulu, imitating Grodmila. She shuddered. 'Ugh!'

'I heard she's still working for Varaminta,' said Aileen, pulling a photo album out of her suitcase. 'Hey, look what I've got here.' The girls huddled round as Aileen opened it up. 'This is my "Lulu" album.'

'Oh wow, I remember that!' exclaimed Lulu as she turned the pages over slowly, the happy memories flooding back. Then came a picture of her with Varaminta. 'Oh no – what's *she* doing in there?'

Aileen winced. 'Ick – yeah, I know, but it's a nice one of you.'

Lulu regarded her sternly.

'Oh, all right,' said Aileen. She pulled the picture out and tossed it in the bin.

'No, hang on,' said Lulu, picking up a pen. 'Varaminta wants a moustache.'

Aileen and Frenchy chuckled as Lulu decorated Varaminta's face. 'Oh here – have some more!' said Aileen, throwing a copy of *Hot* magazine on the bed. 'Plenty of pictures of her in there you can muck about with. Strewth, she's everywhere these days!'

'Yes,' agreed Lulu as she carefully blacked out a Varaminta tooth. 'Seems there's no getting away from her...'

As soon as she said it, Lulu felt a strange lurch in her belly...

Flapjacks and Stuff

Clutching *The Apple Star*, Lulu climbed up to the attic with Frenchy. Dad had gone out again and Aileen, her unpacking finished, was out as well; the girls had the house to themselves. This was important, since what was up here was top secret.

'How d'you know he won't find it?' asked Frenchy.

'Oh, he hardly ever comes up here,' said Lulu. 'Besides,' she added, taking a small key from her pocket and proudly holding it up, 'only I have the key!' She guided Frenchy over to an old wardrobe, unlocked it and swung the doors open. 'Ta-da!'

The wardrobe was the kind with lots of compartments, all crammed with rows of jars and packets. There were exotic honeys, spices, grain flours and nuts. Hanging from the tie rack were ropes of obscure dried fruits, vegetables and roots. Lulu breathed in the heady aroma, so like that of Cassandra's own Aladdin's cave of magical ingredients.

Frenchy popped her bubblegum. 'Wow! Great hiding place, Lu. Hey, I hope your dad's cool about the garden now; I guess telling him about *The Apple Star* and everything is still out of the question?'

Lulu's eyes widened. 'Definitely! OK, I do feel a bit guilty sometimes,' she added, 'but every time I think about Varaminta I remember how lucky he is that I saved him from her. And can you imagine what he'd be like if he found out about the Truth Cookies – or the Cupid Cakes?'

'Ooh, yeah...'

'Besides, you know he'd take this away *instantly*' – Lulu waved *The Apple Star* – 'the minute he realised what a powerful thing it is. He'd be all worried about my safety...come on, French, you know. We've been over this.'

'I know, you're right,' admitted Frenchy. 'Hey, what about his hair!' she added, laughing.

Lulu chuckled too. 'Brilliant, isn't it? I told you I was giving him the Fuzzbooster Flapjacks, didn't I!'

Until recently, Dad's hair had been on the thin side. His forehead had become more and more exposed, like a beach when the tide's gone out. But gradually, to the amazement of everyone except Lulu, the Fuzzbooster Flapjacks produced abundant new waves of thick, lustrous hair.

'He doesn't look too shabby, does he?' said Lulu, proudly. 'Aileen teases him, says he looks *hot*, and she'd better not invite her mates over or they won't be able to keep their hands off him! You know what cracks me up though? The way he does *this* the whole time.' Lulu ran her fingers through her hair. 'He is just *so* pleased with it!'

Frenchy laughed. 'Yeah, I noticed that.'

'You want to know what else I've made?' Lulu reached in and took out two mayonnaise jars filled with sweets. 'Here, check these out.' The sweets in one jar were a deep green colour, while the others were bright red.

'What are they?' asked Frenchy.

Lulu opened *The Apple Star* at the relevant page and showed it to Frenchy.

Frenchy took the book and read aloud: '"Psychic Psours, Medium Sweets; A Mind-Reading Recipe."' She gave a low whistle and read on: '"Although technically two recipes, these count as one, since the one has no effect without the other. The Medium Sweets must be given to the person whose thoughts you need to listen in on; the *transmitter* of the thought-waves. You, as the *receiver* of these thought-waves, will need to eat the Psychic Psours." Oh, this is so excellent! Just think of the fun you could have—'

'Uh-uh-uh!' warned Lulu, wagging a finger. 'Look what it says here: "As with all Level Three recipes, you must exercise *extreme caution* in the use of these two. Do not be tempted to use them for fun! It is a cruel joke and will only lead to trouble."'

'Doh!' said Frenchy, disappointed.

'Cassandra just suggested I make these to keep in reserve,' Lulu continued. 'Being sweets, they can be stored for ages without going off, and they're good to have on standby in case of emergencies.'

'Emergencies? Hey, you're not worrying about Varaminta and Torquil again, are you?' asked Frenchy. Torquil had been hounding Lulu back in the summer, after he and Varaminta had suspected that a magical recipe book was behind Torquil's revelations, and that Lulu was probably the cook.

'Oh no, it's not that. I mean, they don't actually *know* about *The Apple Star*, do they? They've probably decided they were barking up the wrong tree.'

'And Varaminta's got other fish to fry, what with the Fashion Police and everything,' added Frenchy.

'Right. But it can't hurt to have these things, can it?' Even as she said it, Lulu felt a little flutter of nerves in her stomach; just the mention of the V-word was having a strange effect on her lately, though she couldn't understand why. At the same time, she felt an irresistible urge to cook something; she took *The Apple Star* from Frenchy and began flipping through it. 'Oh look – Hush Brownies! Cassandra said those are good to have around too. They're a bit like the Shut-Up Shortbread she gave us – remember?'

'Oh yeah,' said Frenchy. Cassandra's Shut-Up Shortbread had silenced their voices and movements completely. But the effect wore off within minutes; whereas Cassandra merely 'dabbled' in magical recipes, Lulu's *Apple Star* recipes were, she explained, much more powerful. It made Lulu feel very special – if a little nervous.

'Hush Brownies allow you to talk, and they

last much longer – up to eight hours.' Lulu babbled on happily as she foraged in her cupboard for ingredients. 'Brilliant for spying on people! And they also keep for a long time. Now where…oh no, I've just remembered something!'

'What's the matter?'

Lulu scratched her head. 'The recipe uses the root of the Creeping Crillow. I'd have to cut off its legs!'

Frenchy gasped in horror, then remembered this was a vegetable they were talking about. 'Hang on, Lu, it's only a plant!'

'What do you mean, *only* a plant? I love my plants! No, I can't bring myself to do it.'

'Lu, it'll grow back, silly! It's no different from pruning a rose bush, or picking an apple. It's not going to bleed to death or anything.'

'I know, it's just…well, it seems so mean. It wouldn't be able to walk for ages; I'd feel sorry for it.'

'Get it a parasol,' said Frenchy.

Lulu just frowned.

'Oh come on then,' said Frenchy, 'I'll do it!'

'OK,' said Lulu, reluctantly. She put the sweets away and closed up the wardrobe. 'Oh no, wait a minute!' she said, as she picked up *The Apple Star*. 'I just remembered, you mustn't!'

'Why?'

'Nobody else must make the recipes, remember? Or they won't work the way they're supposed to. That includes any preparation.'

'Come on Lu, I don't think—'

'No, I'll do it myself, French. Only I need a few days. To get used to the idea.'

Frenchy rolled her eyes. 'Oh, brother!'

Upside-down Cake

Mrs Pye, the geography teacher, had a broad flat featureless face that was flaky in places. Pie-Face, as she was known, was so dull that her pupils generally ended up about as animated as the rock formations she was so fond of describing in interminable detail. For this reason, Lulu always tried to get some Upside-Down Cake to the staff room in preparation for Monday's double geography. Sometimes Mrs Pye ate it, sometimes she didn't.

'The Ivory Coast is a country in western Africa,' droned Mrs Pye, accompanied by the shufflings and mumblings of a restless class. 'Mostly flat, mountains in the north; number of natural resources, petroleum, diamonds, manganese, etcetera etcetera...'

Lulu's eyes glazed over.

'Key words...endangered species...deforestation...'

'Psst!' hissed Frenchy to Lulu. 'What happened to the Upside-Down Cake?'

'Well sometimes it can take a while to work,' explained Lulu. 'Hang on, I think I see a little sparkle in her eye! That's the first sign...'

'Actually,' said Mrs Pye reflectively, 'now I think about it, there are a lot of really wonderful things exported from the Ivory Coast. Hmm, yes...'

She paused. Zena Lemon snickered at the back. A boy in front of Lulu occupied himself by seeing how much of his pencil he could get up his nose.

'Cocoa!' cried Mrs Pye suddenly, causing the boy to jerk his pencil painfully. Mrs Pye's face opened up, all teeth and eyes where before had been nothing but pie-crust. 'Or cacao, as it is properly known. Without which, of course, there would be no chocolate. In fact, did you know that its scientific name, *Theobroma*, comes from the Greek and means "food of the gods"? Isn't that lovely? *The-o-bro-ma...*' She rolled the syllables around her mouth as if they were made of chocolate.

Lulu caught Frenchy's eye and gave her the thumbs-up sign.

'We also get *diamonds* from the Ivory Coast!' announced Mrs Pye, her voice growing louder. She held up her left hand, displaying the glittering stone in her engagement ring. 'I have one right here; can anyone guess how old it is?'

Several people put their hands up. 'A million years?' said one.

Mrs Pye shook her head. 'Uh-uh. Yes?' she pointed to Galinda Gudvitsa, or Glynnie as she was known to her friends.

'Uh, I think it's something like three billion?' said Glynnie quietly.

'Well done! *Three billion* years; imagine! That's two-thirds as old as the earth itself.'

'Cool!' remarked Frenchy, in rapt attention.

'Finding out about things can be *so* exciting!' Mrs Pye held up her fist as if she were grasping something thrilling out of thin air. Positively flushed with passion for her subject, she went on to make the subject of tropical rainforests more fascinating than Lulu ever thought possible; the thirty minutes whizzed by.

'Now, I'll be testing you all on this at the end of next week,' Mrs Pye rounded off, 'just to be sure that, like Galinda here, you've been paying attention!'

*

'Wow, that was brilliant!' exclaimed Glynnie on their way to the next lesson. 'You know, it's funny, but I could swear all the boring teachers are getting more interesting. Have you noticed? Maybe they've got some kind of new training scheme, sort of "jump-start the dullards"!'

'Mmm, could be,' said Lulu, casting a secret smile in Frenchy's direction. 'By the way, Glyn, where are your glasses?'

Glynnie lit up. 'Oh, I wanted to tell you – it's *unbelievable*! I went to the optician's on Saturday, and guess what? I don't need them any more!'

Lulu slowed down. 'Really?'

'Yeah,' said Glynnie. 'The optician said she'd never seen anything like it! And...hey, I've just realised something!'

'What?'

'You know those headache drinks you gave me?'

'Oh, it's nothing to do with those,' Lulu lied, shaking her head. Secretly, however, she was delighted that the *Apple Star* recipe called Sharp-Eye Shake (which she had pretended to Glynnie was for headaches) had apparently done the trick. A prime target for the Zena Lemon gang, Glynnie had been bullied even more since she had been wearing glasses. But now I've fixed the problem! Lulu congratulated herself. Which, of course, had been the whole point; now Zena and co. would go and pick on someone else for a change.

But no sooner had she thought this, than they

rounded the corner only to be confronted by Zena, together with her best mate Chantrelle Portobello, and their two sidekicks Cara and Mel. They loomed in the corridor like colossal bouncers, blocking the swing doors.

'Hold up, it's teacher's pet,' snarled Zena, curling her lip at Glynnie.

Lulu's bubble burst; she was forgetting that the bullies also hated Glynnie because she was clever.

The giant gobstoppers, as Lulu thought of them, glared down at them, their helmet-like hair and hoop earrings glinting. '"Ooh miss, isn't it something like three billion?"' wheedled Chantrelle Portobello.

Lulu sighed. 'Could you get out of our way, please?'

Zena pushed the door a little way. 'Go on then. We wanna talk to Miss Suck-Up here, innit.'

'Then you can talk to all three of us,' snapped Frenchy, folding her arms. 'What did you have to say?'

'Oo-ooh!' sang all four gang members in response.

'All free of 'em! I'm scared!' taunted Chantrelle.

'Wettin' meself!' smirked Zena. 'Oo-er, better hurry, don't want to get inter trouble, innit!' Together, she and Chantrelle backed into the swing doors and held them open, inviting Lulu and her friends to go through. Cara and Mel stood aside – then before Lulu knew what was happening, she felt herself being shoved forward, while the door came slamming in her face. OW! she cried, reeling back. She heard the cackle of Zena and co. as they thundered away down the corridor in their breeze-block shoes.

Frenchy was sprawled on the floor next to Glynnie, whose nose was streaming with blood. 'Glyn! Are you all right?' said Frenchy, handing her a tissue.

Lulu filled with rage. 'Oh, I am SO going to get back at those girls!'

'Oh yeah?' said Glynnie, the tissue already saturated with bright red blood. Her eyes were glossy with tears. 'How are you going to do that, then? Don't you think we've tried, me and my parents? I tell you, I've just about had it here.'

Frenchie put her arm around her. 'Oh don't say that!'

'It's true – you don't know the half of it! I could bear it when they were always bunking off, but since the school cracked down on that it's been worse than ever!'

Mrs Pye came trotting up to them.

Glynnie glanced over. 'Oh no,' she whispered. 'Listen, don't say anything, OK? It'll only make things worse if she knows.'

'Oh, Galinda, are you all right?' gasped Mrs Pye, handing Glynnie a fresh tissue. She sighed and put her hands on her hips. 'Did Zena Lemon do this?'

'Oh no, Mrs Pye,' insisted Glynnie. 'It was just an accident!'

Mrs Pye turned to Lulu and Frenchy. 'Is this true?'

Lulu badly wanted to tell. But Glynnie was right; Mrs Pye would only give Zena and co. detention, and then who would get the blame for that? Tell-tale Glynnie, that's who. No; there had to be a better way...

'Well?' prompted the teacher.

'Yes, Mrs Pye,' Lulu replied. All feelings of triumph fizzled out of her. 'Just an accident.'

Mighty Muffins

'Well, I mean it!' declared Lulu defiantly as she and Frenchy headed out towards the school gates. 'That Zena and her gang deserve a taste of their own medicine.'

'I know,' agreed Frenchy, taking out two pieces of bubblegum and handing one to Lulu. 'But those muffins were a complete disaster, weren't they?'

Lulu winced. 'Uh, yeah.' Not all of her recipes had been successes. Earlier in the term, she had given Glynnie a Mighty Muffin, a dramatic strength enhancer, in the hope that it would help her defend herself. Unfortunately, Lulu hadn't realised that the Mighty Muffins gave only super-strength, but not the will to fight; Glynnie just endured the bullying with the same quiet resignation. Instead, she had got detention after a series of freak accidents caused by her superhuman strength; she had overturned a desk, ripped out a toilet door, and toppled a shelving unit in the library. Poor Glynnie had had absolutely no idea why.

'Hmm, we need a different approach…' mused Lulu, chewing thoughtfully. At that moment a bus drove past, emblazoned with an ad for *The Fashion Police*, featuring Varaminta in her hallmark peaked cap and mirrored sunglasses, holding up a teapot in a fluffy pink tea cosy. IT'S CRIMINAL! screamed the ad in big white capitals, followed by *The Fashion Police: making the punishment fit the crime, every Thursday, 8.00pm.* Again, Lulu got the same gut-wrenching sensation she kept getting every time she was confronted with some image of Varaminta. *Why* was she still having this effect on her? she wondered, quite forgetting about Zena and co. for a moment. She even let out a little whimper as she twisted her sweatshirt into knots, then took a deep breath as the bus retreated and the pain subsided. Immediately, she was aware of a renewed impulse to cook something. This was becoming a pattern, she'd noticed; the pain followed by this strange urge. Weird, thought Lulu.

Frenchy, however, didn't notice. 'Hey, that's it!' she piped up, jolting Lulu back to the here and now. 'Make the punishment fit the crime; we don't make a recipe for *Glynnie*, at all…we make one for Zena and co. instead!'

'What, all of them?'

Frenchy paused. 'No. Only Zena and Chantrelle; the others are just hangers-on. Now, what could we give them?'

'Never mind that...how do you get them to eat it?' Lulu pointed out. She tried to imagine going up to Zena Lemon and saying, 'Hi, here's a cake I baked for you!' Fat chance.

'Mmm, I see what you mean,' said Frenchy.

They thought for a moment. Suddenly, Frenchy blew a large bubble with her gum; it popped. 'I've got it!' she announced. 'Jump-start the dullards. Give them a taste of their own medicine!'

Lulu frowned. 'How, exactly?'

'Lu, what's the most humiliating thing that could happen to Zena Lemon?'

'Um...'

'Imagine if *she* were the one answering all the questions! If she just couldn't help herself...like Torquil when you gave him the Truth Cookies!'

'French, she'd have to *know* the answers in the first place,' Lulu pointed out.

'Exactly!'

'Oh, you mean give her something to make her intelligent?'

'You got it. The brainier, the swottier, the better!'

A broad smile spread across Lulu's face as she imagined the effect this would have on Zena. She was sure there was something in *The Apple Star* for improving brainpower. 'Oh, French, that's a brilliant idea!' she said at last. 'What would I do without you?'

*

'...So Glynnie goes, "It was just an accident",' said Lulu.

'Oh, poor Glyn,' said Aileen flatly, as they got into the car.

Lulu waited for her to say something more, but Aileen just drove off in silence. This was not like her at all. Where was all the opinionating, where were all the anecdotes from her own schooldays? Aileen would normally have had plenty to say about the episode with Zena Lemon.

Lulu peered at her. 'You OK?'

'What? Oh, yeah, fine.'

But she said nothing more for the entire journey. Lulu was so nonplussed, she couldn't think of a thing to say herself.

'I'll get supper going then, kiddo,' said Aileen, breaking the silence as they arrived home. 'Sausages OK?'

'OK,' said Lulu, staring at Aileen's back as she

disappeared off to the kitchen. Was it something I said? Lulu wondered. She was already feeling as if Aileen was keeping her at arm's length; although Aileen had been her usual bubbly self on Saturday, Lulu had been disappointed when she'd been gone most of the day on Sunday. She hadn't even hung out with Lulu in the evening; claiming she was tired, she had shut herself away in her room. So much for disco parties and midnight feasts, thought Lulu miserably. But when she had complained to Dad, he had just shrugged. 'That's completely normal,' he'd said. 'She's got her own life to lead, and she's only staying here until she gets another flat. Just because she needs a bit of privacy doesn't mean she isn't as fond of you as ever, Noodle.'

Lulu sighed and headed upstairs. She paused outside the door to the guest room – Aileen's room – but its door was tightly shut. No, I mustn't, Lulu told herself. She forced herself to walk past it and into her own room.

She began unpacking her schoolwork, but she couldn't stop thinking about Aileen. She gazed at her picture of Mum on the bedside table, as she often did when she was thinking deeply about something. It was her favourite picture, the Mum-in-Muddy-Wellies one. Lulu no longer talked to Mum's picture the way she used to, but she still turned to it at times like this.

She wondered if something awful had happened yesterday – something Aileen didn't feel able to talk about. Or perhaps she was depressed about not having a boyfriend, and had finally stopped being able to put a brave face on things. Lulu took *The Apple Star* out of its hiding place in a cut-out section of an old encyclopedia, to see if that had any answers. She turned to the introduction to the 'Problems of the Character' section:

> *It is important to think carefully about using these recipes. You must ask yourself, why is this individual behaving in this way? For example, if someone is depressed it may not be the best course of action to give them something to make them happy, such as Cheery Pie. Ask yourself why that person is depressed, and you may find that you would do better to address that problem instead...*

But I *don't* know why Aileen's the way she is! thought Lulu, frustrated. There was only one thing for it; she would have to snoop after all.

Lulu opened the door as gently as possible. The guest room, orderly but overstuffed, was newly filled with Aileen-type smells: hair mousse, face cream. Dolly the mannequin leaned towards Lulu under the weight of two coats, eyeing her reproachfully from beneath her blue lashes. Lulu grimaced and hurried guiltily past, towards the dresser. On it was a pile of books and papers; estate agents' rental lists and a few letters. Among the letters – all boring official ones – was a diploma Aileen had got last year for a psychology course she'd completed. Lulu remembered asking Aileen what she would use it for, but Aileen hadn't seemed sure. Then Lulu's eye was drawn to the wastepaper basket, where there were a couple of scrunched-up pieces of paper. She reached in and picked them up. One was a newspaper cutting…Lulu's heart missed a beat when she saw that it was a recruitment ad for a trainee teaching post. Worse still, it was accompanied by a letter applying for the job advertised – mentioning, among other things, the psychology course.

Lulu stood staring at the crumpled piece of paper, trying to take it all in. She didn't know whether to be shocked and alarmed that Aileen had felt she needed to move on, or relieved that she had changed her mind.

*

Lulu ate her sausages in silence. Her head was full of questions, none of which she could ask, since she wasn't supposed to know about the job application. She felt as if a vast cavern of emptiness had opened up inside her; it reminded her of how lonely she had felt around the cold, sinister Grodmila when she was the housekeeper. 'Are you...going to eat?' she asked eventually.

Aileen usually ate dinner with Lulu, but right now she was busying herself with the clearing up. 'Oh, not all that hungry, kiddo,' she said. 'Maybe I'll have some later.'

Lulu put her fork down. 'Aileen, you're not cross with me about anything, are you?'

Aileen blinked at her. 'Cross with you? Why would I be?'

'I dunno, you're just so...*quiet*! You seem dead miz about something.'

Aileen put the cutlery away and came over to the table. 'Oh, I'm sorry, Lu. I don't mean to be an old wet dishrag. I'm just a bit preoccupied right now with this whole flat business, that's all.' She gave a bright little smile and ruffled Lulu's hair. 'And...well...'

'Yes?'

'I s'pose I do feel it's a bit of an imposition, coming here. Your dad's been so kind, but—'

'It's not an imposition at all!' insisted Lulu. 'Dad's fine with it, and I *love* having you here. At least I would, if...'

'If what?'

'If you were a bit more pally.'

'Well, I'll be able to do that when...when...oh, *soon*, kiddo, OK? When things are more...' She trailed off without finishing her sentence. Then she did something Lulu had never seen her do before; she turned briskly away, and Lulu could have sworn she saw her brush a tear away from her cheek.

Hush Brownies

'Michael, I quit!' cried Costas the gardener, waving his arms in the air. 'Never I see plants like this, makey me crazy!'

'Costas, please—' said Dad.

Lulu tried to be invisible as she slunk past the irate gardener to get some juice out of the fridge. It was already Friday afternoon, but with all the thinking about Aileen and Glynnie this week, she'd quite forgotten that she'd meant to cut off the roots of the Creeping Crillow so as to use them in the Hush Brownies recipe. I *must* do that tonight, she told herself. Anything she could do to calm Costas down a bit…

'No more!' Costas went on. 'I old man, Michael, I can't takey much more. In my day, plants was just plants, you know where you are, eh? Now is all new modern theengs, they jumping out all over tha pless, and go *waawaawaa* in your ear…you know who I blame?'

'Costas—'

49

'All them TV gardeners, that's who I blame! Pah! Everything got to be some gimmick, they not know nothing about real gardening!'

Lulu weaved her way back to the kitchen table to pour her juice. If she had had a tail, it would definitely have been between her legs. It's all my fault, she thought.

'Is all about *money*, Michael! All they care about is making lotsa money showing off in they tight jeans...what's that?'

'That's an extra ten pounds, Costas,' said Dad, holding out the cash.

'Is for me?'

'Yes, Costas.'

Costas fell silent. He looked at the money, then at Lulu's dad. 'Is every week?'

'Every week.'

Costas pocketed the cash and patted Dad on the back. 'You a good man, Michael, you a friend to me. When I say about the money, I didn't mean—'

Dad waved it off. 'Don't mention it, Costas. We want you to stay, don't we, Lulu?'

'Of course!' agreed Lulu. You don't know how much, she thought. The fewer people who knew about her unusual plants, the better.

Dad followed Costas out to the garden and chatted to him for a while, then reappeared through the back door.

'Oh, Dad?' said Lulu. 'Is it OK if I go out with Frenchy tomorrow afternoon? We've got this art project to do for school, and her dad said he'd show us how to use oil paints.'

'Really? That's nice of Jack.'

'Well, he's teaching Frenchy anyway, so he said it was OK if I went along too,' Lulu went on, averting Dad's gaze as she concocted her story. 'It's at his studio in Hackney. Apparently he still works there, even though he's moved back in with Frenchy and her mum.'

'Ah yes,' said Dad, 'I believe he told me. Well, I don't see why not; just wear something old. All right, I'll be in my study for a while, then we'll have some dinner, OK, Noodle?'

'Brilliant!' Lulu grinned; so far so good. She and Frenchy had invented the story about the art project so that they could visit Cassandra. They would walk round from Jack's studio to Cassandra's place after the painting session, on the pretext of a shopping trip.

Boy, do I have a busy weekend ahead, thought Lulu; lots of cooking to do. She would make the Hush Brownies tonight, because after tomorrow's meeting with Cassandra there could be two more recipes to make. Something for Zena and Chantrelle...and possibly something for Aileen.

Lulu sighed; but did she really *want* to help Aileen? She had done as *The Apple Star* had suggested, and looked for the cause of her sadness; she thought she had found it. But having done so put her in a difficult position. If she were to follow Ambrosia May's instructions, she would try to help Aileen follow her dream – yet to do that would mean losing her. But just leaving things as they were didn't seem to be an option either, as Aileen was so obviously unhappy. Lulu hated to admit it to herself, but she realised Aileen would make an excellent teacher. She was brilliant at helping her with her homework; so much better at explaining things than Mrs Pye. Lulu couldn't imagine Aileen ever needing a slice of Upside-Down Cake to liven her up. Why would someone with such a gift want to go on doing housework all day?

Well, better get on with those Hush Brownies for now, Lulu told herself. Perhaps that would take her mind off things. Opening the back door, she saw Sushi creeping warily past the Squirting Squash, giving it a wide berth for fear of a dousing. The phrase 'curiosity killed the cat' sprang to Lulu's mind; she guessed all this just served her right for snooping.

Bracing herself for the task ahead, she took a kitchen knife and went out into the garden and over to the Creeping Crillow. She knelt beside it, grasped it firmly and pulled it out of the ground. 'I'm sorry,' Lulu told the plant, knife in position. Then, shutting her eyes tightly, she cut off its roots. The Crillow didn't squawk or cry; it was completely silent. Lulu, on the other hand, let out a great big howl. She opened one eye, and looked down. The Crillow simply righted itself, and bounced gaily over to a nice shady spot, like a newly shorn lamb. Lulu's cries turned to laughter.

'*Wissy woodle ha ha ha*,' said the Idzumo tree.

'Wissy woodle yourself,' replied Lulu. Then she took the Creeping Crillow root and headed indoors.

Egyptian Spice

Lulu's heart did a little flip at the sight of Cassandra's London taxi cab in the driveway; so ordinary on the outside, yet decked out in blue velvet inside, with a special compartment for the storage of cookies, it was truly unlike any other taxi. The house, too, was deceptively ordinary on the outside – apart, that is, from the Egyptian Pharaoh's head door knocker. Lulu stepped forward, lifted the stubby brass Pharaoh's beard and knocked. It was the first time she had been back to Cassandra's place since the night they'd first met a year before – how long ago that seemed now!

As Lulu and Frenchy waited, they found they were drawn into an intense staring match with a sleek brown cat that was sitting on the window ledge. A moment later, exactly as expected, the Pharaoh's eyelids lifted, revealing a pair of dark eyes.

'Hello, Cassandra!' Lulu grinned boldly; no need for any password this time.

'Aha!' came the caramel-coated voice from inside. The Pharaoh eyes closed, and the door opened to reveal Cassandra in another of the flowing purple robes she favoured so much, a crimson headscarf trailing over her left shoulder, and those same dangly amber and turquoise earrings that she always wore. 'Hello, Lulu!' said Cassandra. 'And...Frenchy, isn't it?'

'Yes,' said Frenchy. 'But I don't mind waiting in the hall,' she added hastily, well aware that she wasn't really supposed to be a part of all this. 'We just had to come together, that's all.'

'I understand,' said Cassandra. 'But, of course, you must join us for some tea. Come!'

Crossing the threshold of the large, darkened room was like entering another world. Even though she'd been here before, Lulu found the heady mix of Egyptian art and the spicy aroma of the many fantastic ingredients stored along the back wall surprised and delighted her all over again. The room was as dark as it had been at night-time, every ounce of daylight blocked out by the heavy curtains, yet it glowed with the warm flickering of candlelight. Cassandra led them to the huge squashy velvet couch, and the girls sank into it.

'Is that your cat outside?' asked Lulu, taking *The Apple Star* out of her bag and resting it in her lap.

'Oh yes, that's Rameses,' said Cassandra as she sat down beside them. 'Have you never met him?'

'No,' said Lulu.

'Well, he's met you,' said Cassandra. 'He'll have checked you out last time you came, but perhaps you didn't notice in the dark. Now: you're worried about someone close to you, aren't you?'

'Uh, yes...' Lulu began, uncertainly. Now that it came to actually doing something to help Aileen, she was once again having serious doubts as to whether she really wanted to.

'It's Aileen,' volunteered Frenchy.

'Ah, Aileen, mmm....the Australian girl.' Cassandra tapped her fingers to her lips. 'I remember her well; pretty thing – zesty! Feisty! She's at a crossroads in her life.'

Lulu blinked at her. Even though she knew about Cassandra's second sight, it always threw her when she came out with things like this. 'Well, yes, I suppose that's one way of putting it—'

'Torn apart!' Cassandra went on dramatically, flinging her arms around and making her earrings jiggle about. 'Wrenched asunder! What is she to do? She must go forward...she must! If she doesn't, her spirit will perish like a withered flower!' She flicked her fingers. 'So. The book?'

'Oh…uh, right.' Lulu reluctantly handed over *The Apple Star*. She gulped. All of a sudden she felt terribly vulnerable; Aileen 'going forward' could only mean one thing – she would have to leave. 'So, uh, if there was some sort of…career opportunity?'

'She must grasp it of course!' said Cassandra, flipping through the pages.

Lulu stared at the pattern on the round brass table in front of her, feeling utterly crushed. 'Actually, I think Aileen's OK now, really,' she announced suddenly.

Frenchy and Cassandra stared at her.

'No, honest, I've just remembered that she was all right last night; much better. So maybe we should discuss the ingredients for…' Lulu paused, distracted by Cassandra's piercing gaze. She lowered her eyes. '…this other recipe, *ahem*—'

'But Lu—' interrupted Frenchy.

Lulu gave her a gentle kick under the table. 'There are these bullies at school, you see, and—'

'Lulu,' said Cassandra gently but firmly, silencing Lulu instantly. 'You should know that you can't deceive me, and I will thank you for not trying.'

Lulu felt tears welling up.

'Lulu, I understand how you feel,' said Cassandra, softening a little. 'But although Aileen cares deeply about you, it seems to be time she broadened her horizons.'

'I said that, didn't I, Lu?' Frenchy reminded her. They had been discussing Aileen all week.

Lulu lowered her head and wiped a tear away.

Cassandra laid *The Apple Star* on the table and stood up. 'Lulu, I think you're about to learn a very important lesson: either you go through life motivated by self-interest...*or* you can help others.'

'But I *have* helped others!' exclaimed Lulu indignantly.

'Mmm, she has,' Frenchy nodded vehemently.

A shadow passed over Cassandra's face. 'Oh Lulu!' She paused for a moment, apparently consumed with emotion. 'If you only knew what it is to *try* to help people, and not be allowed!' She threw up her hands and shook her fists as if in a rage.

Lulu widened her eyes at her, quite startled at this sudden outburst.

Cassandra took a deep breath, leaned on the table and looked Lulu squarely in the eye. 'Don't forget, you have a great gift which you have pledged to use wisely. Believe me, you will never know what it really means to help another, until you have made sacrifices to do so. Search your conscience, Lulu.' She picked up *The Apple Star* again and handed it over. 'This is the recipe I recommend.'

Lulu took the book back.

Cassandra breathed deeply again, in through her nose, then out through her mouth, as if trying to calm down. 'Tea,' she announced at last. 'Tea, tea, tea...' And she wafted out of the room.

Lulu looked at the recipe on the open page: *Chocolate Wishes*.

Fruitcake

'Blimey, what's got into her?' whispered Frenchy. 'Lu, I'm sorry, but if I didn't know better, I'd say our Cassandra was a bit of a fruitcake.'

Lulu frowned at the page, the words a blur. 'No, she's not a fruitcake...but I've suddenly realised I hardly know anything about her. We've never had the chance to talk about anything except this recipe or that plant. It's always these hurried secret meetings, and I worry about being found out.'

'Well, now's your chance, I guess,' said Frenchy. 'Perhaps we can find out more over tea – if she's shaken off her demons. So what's the recipe?'

Lulu read out:

'Chocolate Wishes

A wish come true; these chocolate-coated
morsels will help the eaters to achieve their

goals, by boosting their confidence and
drive. They are especially good for people
who feel that they are in a rut,
going nowhere.'

'Huh! Going nowhere?' Lulu remarked crossly. This stung; it made her feel as if she herself didn't matter.

'Lu,' said Frenchy, reaching for Lulu's arm. 'Do you love Aileen or not?'

'Of course I do!'

'Then you'll want her to do what's right for *her*, even if it's not in your own best interests. Cassandra was right about that, you know.'

Lulu looked away, and found herself staring at the mural on the wall, an image of a man with a dog-headed Egyptian god beside a large pair of scales.

'Look, no one's pretending it's easy,' Frenchy went on. 'If it's any help, I'd find it just as hard if I were in your situation.'

Cassandra returned, apparently calmer, with a tray of tinkling tea glasses. 'Do you know who that is?' she asked Lulu, who was still gazing at the Egyptian mural.

'Well, he does seem vaguely familiar,' said Lulu, welcoming the chance to talk about something else for a moment.

'The jackal-headed god is Anubis,' explained Cassandra, putting the tray down and handing out dishes. 'He is weighing the heart of the deceased man. The heart, you see, was understood to carry a record of all a person's deeds during his lifetime; Anubis will determine if this person's spirit is good enough to enter the kingdom of Osiris, the afterlife. If, however, the heart is weighed down by wrongdoing, it will be consumed by the Devourer of the Dead. The spirit will not survive.'

'Hea-vy,' remarked Frenchy.

Cassandra smiled. 'Yes, I know. The Egyptians' version of hellfire and brimstone! Yet it is wonderfully poetic, don't you think? And after all, isn't life all about weighing up choices? As our Lulu here knows only too well. But you'll get there, my dear,' she added gently, all severity now gone from her voice. 'Give yourself time.' She began pouring the tea.

Her friendlier mood made Lulu feel bolder. 'Cassandra, just now you seemed...well, upset about something.'

Cassandra cleared her throat and sat down. 'Yes, I'm sorry. It's just that every now and then, I...do you have time for a story?'

'Yes,' replied both girls without hesitation.

'I was not much younger than you when it

happened. In those days we lived in a village on the Atlantic coast of Morocco. The wind blew night and day without rest, sprinkling salt on the walls, so they glistened like rock candy. Some said the ceaseless wind could drive you crazy; "the wind blew through his ears," they'd say. I wasn't fully aware of my second sight until I had a dream when I was about twelve, predicting a shipwreck on nearby Falcon Island. I ran down to the harbour to alert my Uncle Ali and cousin Omar, who were both fishermen...'

Lulu was transported; she could almost taste the salt on her lips, hear the scream of the gulls as she pictured the young Cassandra weaving her way through the bustling Moroccan harbour.

'I urged them to gather men together to go to the island,' Cassandra went on, 'to do anything they could to avert the disaster...or at least have their boats ready there so they might rescue some of the crew when it happened. But they just looked at me as if I was mad. You see, Falcon Island got its name because it was inhabited only by falcons. A two-thousand-year-old legend said it was cursed; any human who set foot on its shores would be pecked to death by the birds.

'So Omar teased me, saying, "The wind blew through her ears". I pleaded with them, saying it was only an old wives' tale about the falcons. But they didn't take me seriously, and nobody went.' Cassandra bowed her head. 'There was indeed a storm that night...next morning there were reports that a cargo ship had been seen near Falcon Island. Then it had disappeared.'

'Oh, my...' Lulu trailed off. Now Cassandra's outburst made perfect sense; just like Lulu herself, Cassandra had a special gift – yet when she had tried to use it, she had been cruelly rendered helpless. And to this day she had to live with the knowledge that people had died because of it.

Lulu couldn't help feeling a little ashamed. How small and insignificant her own worries about losing Aileen seemed now.

Chaste-tree Berries

Cassandra found the ingredients Lulu needed, and was just finishing wrapping them when a strange sound came from outside; a low wail like a waning siren.

Cassandra froze.

'What's that?' asked Lulu.

'That's the cat, Rameses – it means we have a visitor...someone unwelcome. Rameses screens my visitors, you know, and he's never been wrong about anyone yet. And...'

'Yes?'

'I have a bad feeling about this one,' said Cassandra. Her face bore this out; it seemed to have turned quite grey.

The doorbell rang, an eerie chiming that made Lulu jump. Cassandra picked up something that looked like a TV remote control. She pointed it at the back wall, where all the jars of ingredients were. Immediately, sections of the wall began to move, and soon they had rotated through 180 degrees, leaving a perfectly blank wall. Then Cassandra pointed the remote at her honey cabinet and the extraordinary giant fridge with a door like an Egyptian sarcophagus, both of which became concealed, boxed in by fake walls.

'Wow,' said Lulu.

'Just like you, Lulu, I'm sworn to secrecy. This is my disguise.'

The doorbell rang again, and Rameses let out a loud hiss of disapproval. Lulu's imagination began to run wild. 'It's not...someone after me, is it?'

'No,' said Cassandra. 'I know exactly who it is. Come...down here.' She escorted Lulu and Frenchy down some steps into a basement room. 'You had better leave the back way...there's a gate at the end of the garden that leads to a footpath – go!'

Lulu and Frenchy did as they were told, and ran out into the garden. Fallen leaves whirled in the gathering wind under the iron-grey sky.

'*Ooh-hoo-hoo! Got to hurry-hurry-hurry!*' whispered a strange voice.

'Aargh!' squealed Lulu, clutching Frenchy, who was also paralysed with fear.

'*Wah-wah quindy calloo-oo!*'

Still clutching each other, the girls looked around to see where the voice came from.

'Oh, look!' said Frenchy, pointing. 'It's only the Idzumo tree!'

Lulu clasped her chest. 'Oh good grief! Let's get out of here!'

'Which way?' asked Frenchy, casting her eye around for the gate.

Straight ahead was a lattice screen hung with creepers, with an arch in the middle. 'Through there!' said Lulu. They dashed under the arch and into Cassandra's vegetable patch. Barely able to register the extraordinary array of plants there, Lulu spotted what looked like the gate, half hidden by vegetation. She urged Frenchy towards it. It was only when they were actually upon it that Lulu realised she recognised the plant that was growing around the gate. 'Stop!' she ordered, but it was too late.

'Aargh!' cried Frenchy, for as she pushed the plant aside, it shot a tendril out and wrapped itself around her arm.

'Oh, no, it's a Dum'zani plant!' gasped Lulu.

Frenchy tugged, trying to free herself, and another tendril clamped onto her. 'A – a what?'

'Don't move!' ordered Lulu. 'You've got to stay perfectly still; any movement only makes it cling tighter. It's a Dum'zani plant; you know the one I used for the Cupid Cakes, that likes to hug people...I should have noticed the blue cobs! Oh, I'm sorry...'

'Well, how do I get out then?' squeaked Frenchy.

Lulu put her fingers to her temples. 'OK, think, think...'

Thunder began to rumble in the darkening sky. Big, heavy drops of rain began to fall.

'What we need is the Anti-Dote,' said Lulu. 'The recipe, it's a sorbet...'

'Well, great!' said Frenchy sarcastically. 'Just nip down to the corner shop then, and ask for some!' She moved her arm slightly, causing another tendril to wrap itself around her. 'Aargh! Oh Lu, get me out!'

'I know!' said Lulu suddenly, and she turned around and started examining the plants in Cassandra's garden. 'If I can just find *one* ingredient...'

The wind howled, and along with it Lulu thought she heard a man's voice say, '*Who's out there?*' Seconds later came another, ethereal voice: '*Who's out there got to hurry-hurry-hurry!*'

'Ooh, hurry up!' pleaded Frenchy.

Lulu's heart pounded. 'I'm thinking, I'm thinking! There was cankerblossom...no, no...berries...yes! A Chaste tree!' Lulu grabbed handfuls of the familiar small black berries from a nearby shrub and began rubbing them into the base of the Dum'zani plant. 'Just tell me if you feel the *slightest* slackening,' she hissed.

The rain began to pelt harder, plastering Lulu's hair to her head. Now she could hear the ominous splodging sounds of approaching footsteps in the sodden leaves... 'Oh my...anything yet?' she squeaked.

'Um...I think, maybe...'

Lulu grabbed some more of the purple berries and smooshed them into the roots with her sodden, blackened hands. Glancing up, she thought she noticed the plant slacken slightly.

Splodge, splodge came the footsteps, nearer and nearer. Then a man's voice called out, 'Hey, you!'

'Hey you, whatcha gonna do-oo-ooo!'

Frenchy whimpered.

Lulu stood up and used her foot to grind the squashed berries deeper still into the base of the plant. At last, it loosened its grip just enough for Frenchy to free herself – but now a large man appeared through the arch. He pushed into the thicket of the Dum'zani plant, reaching for Frenchy's other arm, but she just slipped out in time. The plant, stimulated by the violent movement despite the effect of the Chaste-tree berries, clamped onto the man's arm. He managed to get hold of Frenchy's sleeve with his other hand, but couldn't free himself and the more he struggled, the more tendrils shot out to entangle him. Frenchy wrenched her sleeve free of his grip, and the two girls bolted through the gate and down the footpath. Glancing back, Lulu could just make out a flailing arm amid the shaking branches of the Dum'zani plant.

Chocolate Wishes

'Lulu, I'm so glad you're all right!' said Cassandra, when she phoned Lulu later. 'I'm sorry about what happened this afternoon.'

'Well, I'm glad you're all right too,' said Lulu. 'But who *was* that?'

'Someone who thinks they can take everything away from me...an occupational hazard, I'm afraid, hence my "disguise"!' said Cassandra, breezily. Lulu couldn't help thinking she sounded a little *too* breezy – as if trying to make light of the afternoon's events. 'I had thought that visit would be somewhat later,' Cassandra went on. 'Even I don't always foresee things exactly as they turn out...'

Lulu thought about the man who had chased after her and Frenchy; she shuddered. She remembered seeing a badge on his sleeve; a golden fish-tailed horse with a crown above it. 'But what was that—'

'Just *don't worry* about it, Lulu,' Cassandra said

firmly. 'Everything's all right now. You must get on and make those recipes; promise me you will?'

'Well…yes, I suppose…'

'Good,' said Cassandra. 'It's important that you do. I hope it all goes well…goodbye.'

Lulu sat staring at her Mum-in-Muddy-Wellies picture for a while, thinking about Cassandra, her psychic cat and her transformer home. 'How can *anyone* get used to an occupational hazard like that?' she wondered aloud. She guessed such things must happen to Cassandra all the time – but what a strange life she must lead!

Lulu sighed, and decided she might as well do as she was told and get on with making the Chocolate Wishes. Dad was happy to leave her to it, since cooking had become such a regular weekend routine for Lulu. And Aileen was out looking at flats. Lulu had seen her that morning, briefly; once again, Aileen had been pleasant…and distant as the hills. All the fizz gone out of her, like a glass of flat soda.

Before long, Lulu found she was engrossed in the task of cooking and had quite forgotten about the intruder. She emptied the contents of a small bag marked 'Honeydew' into her mixing bowl; the little white crystals tinkled against the earthenware like silver bells. Cassandra had called them 'the tears of the

Tamarisk tree'; these were the original 'manna from heaven' spoken of in the Bible; 'And what could be more divinely inspirational than that?' Cassandra had remarked.

As she worked, Lulu lost herself in the folklore associated with each ingredient. It was this effect that made her find the recipes so compelling; in her imagination she became the figures in the stories. One moment she was an Israelite trudging through the heat and dust of the Sinai desert, picking up the magical droplets of manna from the ground. Then she became the man from another of Cassandra's tales, who tried to run away from the destiny he dreamed of as he slept in the boughs of the Yellow-Flowered Zwart-Storm tree. The butter made from the nuts of this tree was to help the eater embrace his aspirations.

Now Lulu added dried Quicksilver berries, which resembled little beads of mercury, and which conferred likewise mercurial qualities in the eater, helping him to scale new heights with the use of the mind. She transformed into the Roman god Mercury, soaring aloft on winged sandals.

She added the Odin's Mead, a fermented honey drink associated with the great Norse god, and became a deity of Asgard herself, holding out a bowl to catch the magical drink spat out by Odin as he swooped overhead in the form of a huge eagle. It was known as the Mead of Poetry. 'There is not a single field of endeavour', it explained in *The Apple Star*, 'that is not furthered by beauty in one's words. But take care to add *exactly* the correct amount; a drop too much of this powerful brew can cause one to spout endless poetry, which could be disastrous!' Last of all Lulu added the crushed Velvet Flower, which was sacred to the Greek hunter-goddess Artemis and therefore meant to help females pursue their goals. And as Lulu mixed everything together, she imagined herself as the fleet-footed Artemis, chasing through the Olympian forests after wild beasts with her bow and arrow.

Lulu spread the thick paste out on some parchment and cut it into squares. Now came the chocolate. 'In its purest form, chocolate will stimulate mind, body and spirit,' Cassandra had said, reminding Lulu of what Mrs Pye had taught. Lulu melted the rare Madagascan chocolate very slowly, as instructed, then carefully poured the velvety, fragrant dark fluid over the squares.

Then came the moment Lulu always dreaded: what Ambrosia May called The Pang. The Pang came when you stopped concentrating on what you were doing (or, in Lulu's case, losing yourself in the stories) and noticed how desperately – how longingly! – you

wished to try out the recipe yourself. It happened to Lulu every time, and she still hadn't got used to it. So now she always made sure she had something to hand for emergency consumption. Lulu sat down and ate an ordinary everyday chocolate bar, sighing with relief as The Pang subsided.

But the other pang, the one she got every time she thought of losing Aileen...that was very much still there.

*

'Hi Aileen, how are you?' Lulu almost shrieked as Aileen came bursting through the front door, dripping wet. What perfect timing; Lulu had only just finished making the Chocolate Wishes and put everything away – including, most importantly, *The Apple Star*.

'Soaked!' Aileen responded wearily, peeling off her sodden denim jacket. 'Gotta get into some dry things.'

'I'll put the kettle on!' Lulu announced.

Aileen smiled wanly. 'Oh, perfect,' she croaked. 'A cup of tea would go down a treat!'

'Yup, we Poms are good for something, I guess,' joked Lulu. In better times, Aileen would always tease Lulu about 'you Poms', and Lulu was interested to see if she would be amused.

But Aileen was already halfway up the stairs, apparently unaware of her little quip. Depressed, thought Lulu; definitely not her usual self. She headed eagerly back into the kitchen, where she quickly arranged the Chocolate Wishes in a little raffia basket she had lined with purple silk. Despite her worries, she felt quite excited now.

'Present,' said Lulu, holding out the basket of chocolates for Aileen upon her return. 'I made them.'

'You made these?' said Aileen. Clearly impressed, she even seemed to perk up a little.

'Yeah!'

'That's great, kiddo. Thank you!' She gave Lulu a hug and a kiss. 'You are clever. Here, let's have some.'

'Oh, not for me, thanks,' said Lulu. 'I'm...full.'

'Nonsense!' said Aileen, holding out the basket. 'You're never too full for *chocolate*. Here!'

'No, really!' insisted Lulu. 'I've...actually got a bit of a tummy ache. But you're not to share them with anyone else either, understand? They're *especially* for you.'

Aileen shrugged. 'OK.' She lifted one to her mouth.

'Wait!' said Lulu quickly, grabbing Aileen's arm. Aileen cast her a worried glance. 'They're special...*wishing* chocolates,' Lulu added, hoping she

cheerfully. 'Maybe she's busy filling out a job application forms.'

Although this was of course the object of the exercise, the thought of it only made Lulu more miserable. 'Yeah, that occurred to me too,' she said heavily.

Lulu decided to get on with making the Nuggets; she would lose herself in the stories again, as she had with the Chocolate Wishes, and that would take her mind off Cassandra and Aileen.

After making the base mixture of bean curd and oil, she added the dried Salmon of Knowledge Eggs. Cassandra had assured Lulu these would only make the Nuggets taste salty, not fishy. As Lulu stirred them in, she was transported to the magical Ireland inhabited by giants and little people. She became the legendary hero, Finn M'Coul, sitting in a cave and roasting the Salmon of Knowledge for his giant master, who threatened to cut off his head if he took one morsel for himself. But when Finn scalded himself on the fish he sucked his thumb...and great wisdom was bestowed on him. 'There really is a salmon pool in Ireland,' Cassandra had explained, 'and around it grows a very special kind of hazelnut tree. It is by feeding on the nuts that fall from these trees that the salmon gain wisdom which is then concentrated in their eggs.' Lulu pictured the idyllic scene: a glade on squiggly-branched trees dropping their green-jacketed nuts into the glistening water, to be swallowed by swishing iridescent fish as big as her leg.

Lulu added a special kind of Wormwood Seed, and now she became a boldly painted Aztec woman doing a tribal dance around a huge fire, her head adorned with this brain-stimulating plant. She could almost hear the pounding of drums as she pictured the scene of the ancient Mexicans celebrating their festival of the goddess of salt. Fancy having a goddess of salt! she thought.

Next came the chopped preserved Medusa Root. This was associated with Athena, the Greek goddess of wisdom, and so called because it resembled the snake-headed gorgon of that name. Lulu became Athena, springing fully formed from the head of her father, Zeus, and venturing forth with her shield, carved with a Medusa head to ward off evil.

All this vivid imagery provided a welcome distraction, but it soon receded as Lulu went about the monotonous task of rolling the mixture into balls, dipping them in egg and breadcrumbs and then frying them. Now the thoughts of Cassandra came flooding back; she stared reproachfully at the telephone, which remained stubbornly silent.

*

'Oh, it's *them* lot serving, we'll be here all day!' complained Zena loudly as she drew nearer in the lunch queue. 'Come on, I'm starvin'!'

Good, thought Lulu. After collecting the carefully wrapped Nuggets from her locker, Lulu had caught sight of Glynnie's parents heading for the principal's office, faces like stone: there wasn't a moment to lose. It was time to vanquish the giants – outsmart them like Finn M'Coul. As the two looming figures approached, Lulu dived under the counter to replenish her tray with chicken nuggets…as well as exactly twelve Nuggets of Information, clearly identifiable by their different shape. She grimaced at the flabby lumps, which looked about as appetising as day-old fish and chips; hurriedly, she took a little salt-shaker from her pocket and shook it over them. Although it looked just like salt, the stuff inside was actually something Cassandra had given her called 'Spritz', especially for making the nuggets look more appealing.

Glynnie appeared in the line, looking more miserable than ever. 'Oh Lu, I didn't realise you were monitoring. I…was actually hoping to talk to you.'

Lulu paused, spatula in hand. 'Hey, Glyn, is everything OK? I saw your parents just now.'

Glynnie's eyes glazed with tears. 'Yes, well, they've made up their minds…I really am leaving.'

'Ow, come ON!' yelled Zena.

Lulu quickly filled Glynnie's plate. 'We'll talk later, OK?' she reassured her, before the line swept along and now she was confronted with Zena and Chantrelle. Glancing down, Lulu was delighted to see that the Spritz had now transformed her pallid lukewarm blobs into crispy, golden cutlets, sizzling happily on the hot tray. 'There you go!' she beamed cheerfully as she dished them out, six each. 'Enjoy!'

Zena sneered back. ''Bout time,' she snapped.

'Yes,' Lulu answered under her breath. 'It certainly is.'

'Two weeks,' said Glynnie, when Lulu and Frenchy joined her to eat their own lunch. 'That's how long my parents are giving it; if things haven't changed by then, I'm out. So basically I'm going; there's no way anything's going to change before then.'

'It might, Glyn!' said Frenchy, patting her on the shoulder. 'It really might...'

At the next table sat Zena and Chantrelle, who had both finished their lunch. Lulu was glad to see that their plates had not a scrap of food left on them. She leaned closer, to listen in on their conversation. As usual, the hangers-on were there, Cara and Mel. ''Ere, y'know woss on telly again tonight?' said Cara. 'That programme *The Fashion Police*. I can't wait – I missed it last week.'

'Oh it's a good one!' said Mel. 'You gonna watch it Zena?'

Zena considered this for a moment. 'Well, I might not have time; I'm thinking I'd quite like to find out more about the indigenous peoples of the Ivory Coast and their respective customs.' As soon as the words were out of her mouth, Zena's eyes darted this way and that in a look of mild shock.

Cara and Mel stared at her, slack-jawed. 'Yer wot?'

Zena, flaming with embarrassment at the spectacular uncool-ness of what she had just said, set her jaw into its usual sneer with visible effort. 'I mean...*nah*, course ah'm gonna watch it, isn't it? I mean, aren't I? I mean...I've got to go!'

She jumped up, and was quickly joined by Chantrelle. Lulu just heard her saying eagerly to Zena, 'Hey, I'm really fascinated with that subject too!' as they were leaving the dining hall.

'Woss got into 'er all of a sudden?' said Mel, looking as if her brain might implode any minute.

'I dunno, but she sounded right snotty,' said Cara.

Lulu caught Frenchy's eye, smiled and gave her the thumbs-up. Result.

Pork Scratchings

'This is the Leicestershire home of the Scratching family. Mr and Mrs Scratching are preparing their dinner in the kitchen. Their teenage daughter, Porchia, is getting ready to go out for the evening with a friend, while her two younger brothers play in the garden.'

As the TV voice-over introduced the Scratchings against a background of chirpy music, the camera showed each family member in turn, going about their activities.

'A typical English family, doing nice, typical things on this pleasant English evening, you might think...but wait!' The music, and the voice, switched to a sombre, dramatic mood. 'You would be *very, very wrong*! For every last member of this family is guilty of a crime so heinous, that their neighbours have had no option but to report them to...THE FASHION POLICE!'

And the camera cut to a severe-looking woman dressed in a very sharply tailored version of a police uniform, complete with mirrored sunglasses, peaked cap and high-heeled black patent boots: Varaminta le Bone.

'Aargh!' cried Lulu, half-hiding her face with a pillow. 'Those poor people!'

Aileen cried out too, clutching on to Lulu. 'Oh, just look at her!'

Lulu didn't let on, but the sight of Varaminta was making her stomach turn. She knew it would, but had decided she really needed to get over what seemed to be some kind of phobia. Since Dad would be out all evening, this was the ideal opportunity to give herself extended exposure to Varaminta, the way people afraid of spiders overcame their fear by handling tarantulas. And since everyone at school was talking about the show, she was also very curious.

Next, the three 'police women' stormed in on the Scratching household. 'Ugh! I cannot *believe* you're wearing rhinestone jeans!' shrieked Varaminta at poor old Mrs Scratching, who up until that moment had probably thought she looked quite hip and sassy. 'At your age!' Varaminta barked. 'Have you never *heard* the phrase "mutton dressed as lamb"?'

Lulu sank further into her seat, peeking from behind the pillow. 'Oh no, I don't think I can watch this!' But like a horror movie, *The Fashion Police* had a hold over her that she couldn't quite tear herself away from. She went on cowering in her seat, her skin crawling as Varaminta and her two accomplices went on to demolish not just the clothes of the entire Scratching family, but their taste in interiors and leisure activities as well. At last Varaminta whipped out a set of handcuffs and clamped them onto Mr Scratching's wrists. *Click! Click! Click!* went further restraints, until every family member was cuffed. 'We arrest you on charges of crimes against fashion!' Varaminta announced gloatingly. 'Take 'em away!'

'"Fashion Police" indeed! "Fascist Police" more like it!' exclaimed Aileen.

In spite of the crassness of the Varaminta show, and the twisting in her belly that refused to go away, Lulu took some comfort from the fact that Aileen actually seemed to be back to her old self at last.

Somehow, they managed to sit through the entire programme, during which the handcuffed Scratching family were removed to the high street with Varaminta. Finally, having served their sentence in tasteful stores of Varaminta's choice, they were re-installed in their newly purged home, looking about as comfortable in it as a seven-year-old boy in a three-piece suit. Gone were the trainers and tracksuits, replaced by sleek colour-coordinated outfits in muted tones.

'Now, don't do it again, understand?' demanded Varaminta at the end, slapping a truncheon in her hand as she paraded up and down, inspecting the line-up.

'No, Miss,' chorused the Scratching family meekly.

'And *try* to lose some weight,' she barked at the unfortunate Porchia. 'I mean, I've done the best I could, but really! With a backside the size of Wales, there's only so much one can do!'

The poor girl looked as if she wanted the ground to swallow her up.

Aileen got up and turned the TV off. 'Well, I guess Varaminta's made progress of a sort,' she remarked.

'Progress?!' exclaimed Lulu. 'Are you kidding?'

'I mean, at least she's not pretending to be a *nice* person any more! Like she used to when she was with your dad. She's owned up; she knows she's horrible, and she's going with it.'

'Well, that's true,' said Lulu, feeling better already now that the TV was off. 'And getting herself a whole new set of fans into the bargain, by the sound of it.' *The Fashion Police* was hitting the headlines as a TV ratings blockbuster, and Varaminta was beginning to gain some of the fame and fortune she craved so desperately. This could only be good news for Lulu too, since Varaminta had well and truly moved on from pursuing her for *The Apple Star*. So why she still got this nasty sensation that Varaminta was out to get her, Lulu couldn't figure at all. She'd better get busy in the kitchen; that would make her feel better...

*

'Hello, my name Andreas. Costas, he send me,' said the rather short, stout man on the doorstep. Lulu saw him talking to her dad as she was coming downstairs for breakfast.

'Ah yes, that's right,' said Dad. 'Costas called the other day, he told me about you; well, come in. I hope he's OK?'

'Oh yes, he OK,' said Andreas as he came into the hallway. 'Just he have bad cold in the chest, making to cough all of the time. But I good gardener,' he added, beaming, 'I know how to do.'

Yes, except you've never had a garden quite like ours to deal with, thought Lulu, nervously. Still, at least the Crillow wouldn't be creeping for a while; she just hoped the Idzumo tree and the Squirting Squash would behave themselves.

'I'm sure you do, Costas wouldn't recommend you otherwise,' said Dad. 'Lulu, show Andreas through to the garden, will you? I've just got to finish getting ready.'

'OK,' said Lulu. She paused as she took in the ruddy face, framed with straggly facial hair. 'Have you been before?' she asked.

'Not here, no,' said Andreas. 'But I good gardener, you be happy!'

Lulu let Andreas out into the garden, then went into the kitchen and had breakfast. After which, this being Friday, she prepared her final batch of Nuggets of Information for Zena and Chantrelle, ready for today's test. She was glad this was the last day; it had been quite a lot of work. But Lulu was very encouraged by how things were going; every day that week, she and Frenchy had succeeded in getting the two bullies served with the magical Nuggets which, as they were delicious almost to the point of being addictive, had been their choice every time. What was more, all the signs suggested that the Nuggets were working; Zena and Chantrelle had become strangely quiet, apparently too interested in studying to have time for bullying.

Lulu was just putting the wrapped Nuggets into her backpack when Dad wandered into the kitchen, studying the mail that had just arrived. He glanced at Lulu, noticing the way she eyed Andreas uneasily through the kitchen window. 'Don't worry about your plants, Noodle, it's just for one day,' he said. 'Although my botanist friend would—'

'No!' insisted Lulu.

Dad rolled his eyes, and turned his attention back to the mail. 'Oops, shouldn't have opened that one,' he said, dropping a letter onto the kitchen table. 'It's for Aileen; can't get used to having someone else around... Do tell her it was a mistake, won't you, and that I'm not snooping through her mail!' He glanced at his watch. 'Oh, is that the time? I must get going...see you tonight, love!' He planted a peck on Lulu's head, then hurried off to work.

Lulu looked at the opened letter that sat invitingly on the table in front of her. Aileen had just been getting into the shower when Lulu came downstairs; she wouldn't be down yet. It was just too tempting; Lulu reached over and took the letter out of its envelope. Her face tingled as she saw the familiar logo for the education authority that had advertised the job, and the note which confirmed the receipt of Aileen's application, saying they would be in touch in the near future.

Lulu hurriedly slipped the letter back into its envelope and set it aside. So Aileen *had* applied... Oh well, thought Lulu; she still might not get the job.

*

Lulu stared at the geography test paper, suddenly painfully aware that she'd spent hardly any time revising. There had just been too much on her mind over the past two weeks; what with Cassandra and her mysterious visitor, and Aileen and the Chocolate Wishes – not to mention the whole Zena versus Glynnie thing coming to a head – schoolwork had definitely been lagging behind. Got to concentrate...oh, why didn't I have some Nuggets of Information too? Lulu berated herself. She could certainly use a little brain-boosting right now. Too busy rescuing other people, that was the problem – like some daft misguided superheroine. And wasn't it the fate of all superheroes and heroines to be useless at their day jobs? What Lulu had yet to prove was whether she was even up to scratch in the superheroine department.

Yet there was at least one very encouraging sign; as she glanced over at Zena and Chantrelle, Lulu saw that the two of them had their heads down and were scribbling furiously. Fantastic! Cara and Mel, in contrast, looked about as fired up as a damp box of matches; yes, it would be *very* interesting to see the results of this test. Especially since Glynnie would be leaving in just one week unless something dramatic happened.

Pink Pudding Face

Monday morning. Mrs Pye entered the room, the usual scowl of contempt on her pasty pie-crust face. 'Now, I've marked your test papers over the weekend, and I have…some *observations*.' She paused for effect, and gazed around the classroom.

Oh boy, here we go, thought Lulu nervously; she felt sure she was about to be singled out for doing so badly.

'Zena and Chantrelle,' said Mrs Pye. Lulu held her breath; *surely* they hadn't fouled up – not after all the work they'd done? She snuck a surreptitious glance at them; they didn't seem to know where to put their faces. 'Never, in all my years of teaching,' Mrs Pye went on gravely, '…have I ever witnessed such a stunning transformation! Girls, please, come forward.'

Zena and Chantrelle remained paralysed in their seats, awestruck. Cara and Mel made stifled little giggles.

'Yes, I'm talking to *you*!' insisted Mrs Pye. 'Zena

Lemon and Chantrelle Portobello – come!' She beckoned them over.

Zena and Chantrelle had no choice but to join Mrs Pye at the front of the class. They did so with stooping shoulders and dragging feet. Brilliant! thought Lulu. She glanced over at Glynnie, who stared in amazement.

Mrs Pye's flaky face creased into a smile as she put her arms around the two giantesses. 'Now, usually, I have to call you two up to the front of the class because of bad behaviour. But this time, it is because you have done exceptionally well. Congratulations, I knew you had it in you! In fact I am so delighted with your work that I'm going to reward you!'

'Reward' – ha! Lulu had to stifle a grin at the sight of Zena and Chantrelle's shell-shocked faces. This was just too perfect!

Mrs Pye handed out two huge shiny badges to the girls. 'You have proved to the rest of us just what can be achieved when you put your mind to it! And I know you haven't been cheating…this was timed work, in the classroom – I saw it all. Well, put them on,' she urged, pointing to the badges.

Zena's pudding face turned pink. She tried hard to cover her embarrassment with a sarcastic smirk.

'Yeah, go on!' urged some of the boys, loving every minute of this. Encouraged by them, the usually rather spineless Cara and Mel joined in. 'Put 'em on! Put 'em on!' they chanted rhythmically, banging their rulers on their desks.

Zena glared over at Chantrelle, a look that said 'I ain't doing this by myself'. Then the two of them went ahead and pinned the big round badges to their sweaters. On the badges were the words 'Top of the Class!'

A huge cheer rose up, far louder than it would have been if it were one of genuine congratulation. For there wasn't a single class member who wasn't thoroughly enjoying Zena's and Chantrelle's squirming.

'All right, that's enough,' called Mrs Pye feebly over the din, but the applause only grew more raucous, accompanied by hoots and whistles. Finally, Zena could stand it no longer. She turned and stomped out of the classroom, slamming the door behind her.

Mrs Pye's jaw dropped. 'Well, whatever is the matter with her?' she asked Chantrelle.

Chantrelle shrugged. 'Don't know, Mrs Pye.'

*

'*Fashion Police* tonight,' Lulu heard Zena announce to Chantrelle three days later, as they packed up to go home from school. 'Can't wait!'

'I ain't watching it,' said Chantrelle dismissively.

Lulu and Frenchy trailed closely behind them as they left the building, curious as to what would happen now that the effect of the Nuggets had worn off.

'Wodger mean, you ain't watchin' it, eh?' challenged Zena. 'You always watch it.'

'Look I just ain't, all right?'

Lulu grinned at Frenchy; from the moment that Chantrelle failed to show solidarity with Zena after she'd stormed out of the lesson, a rift seemed to be widening between these two. Lulu's amusement turned to dread, however, when they reached the school gates. She clutched Frenchy's arm. 'Oh good grief, look at that!' she whispered, nodding at a black van parked across the street. On its side was a familiar logo: a golden fish-tailed horse with a crown above it.

Frenchy froze. 'That man at Cassandra's...'

'Exactly,' said Lulu. She linked arms with Frenchy and they began walking briskly, keeping close to Zena and her gang. The van pulled out and began to follow them; all the more reason to go a different way than usual, thought Lulu. She could always send Aileen a text message saying she'd be a little late. But now the Zena Lemon gang slowed down as they approached the entrance to the local park, where they usually hung out after school.

'Look, I told you, I've got homework to do!' Chantrelle protested.

'Woss got into you?' Zena challenged angrily.

Chantrelle gave her a withering look. 'It's what we're *s'posed* to do, Zena!'

While there was safety in numbers, Lulu was not comfortable waiting around for the argument to be over with; the van had now parked nearby and two hefty blond men in black overalls had emerged and were approaching. Lulu and Frenchy shifted to a nearby group of boys heading towards the bus stop and tried to lose themselves among them instead.

But now this group also came to a standstill, attracted by the conflict between Zena and Chantrelle, which had escalated into a full-blown punch-up.

'Whoo! Catfight, *yeah*!' cried one of the boys, and soon they were all whooping and cheering.

Not knowing what else to do, Lulu and Frenchy stayed close to the group and watched. Lulu wished the men would go away. Not only did they make her extremely uncomfortable, but they were spoiling what should have been a great moment – the one that might well signal the beginning of the end of Zena's gang.

Her prayers were answered when a policewoman appeared. 'All right, break it up!' she commanded, striding towards Zena and Chantrelle.

Lulu caught a glimpse of the men as they retreated a little way from the scene, apparently uncomfortable in the presence of the police. Seizing her chance, Lulu grabbed Frenchy's hand and made a dash in the other direction, heading into the park.

*

'We don't actually *know* they were after us, Lu, do we?' Frenchy pointed out at breaktime the next day.

'Well, no,' Lulu had to admit. 'But it certainly felt that way; I'm keeping a sharp eye out for those guys from now on.'

Frenchy had to agree. 'Still, at least they don't know where either of us lives,' she said. 'I mean, as far as we know.'

'We'll have to be careful if we want it to – *ow!* – stay that way...' Lulu doubled up as she caught sight of Varaminta's face leering from the front of the magazine a group of girls were poring over; that lurching sensation in her stomach again. So her attempt at aversion therapy by watching *The Fashion Police* hadn't worked, after all.

'You OK?' asked Frenchy.

'Oh yeah, fine,' said Lulu, straightening up. She couldn't even tell Frenchy about this; it was too embarrassing. But the problem was, if anything, getting worse; Lulu actually found herself wishing she could go to the doctor about it. Perhaps she really had developed a serious phobia, and needed a psychiatrist...or maybe *The Apple Star* had something for curing phobias...? But then if it did, she would probably need Cassandra, and Cassandra had very inconsiderately gone and disappeared. How dare she!

Her thoughts were interrupted by a flushed and excited Glynnie, who rushed over and sat beside them. 'Listen, guys, you'll never believe it, but it looks as if I won't be leaving after all!'

In spite of her worries, Lulu couldn't help being swept along by Glynnie's exuberance and gave her a hug. 'Oh Glyn, that's fantastic!'

'I talked things over with my mum and dad last night,' Glynnie went on merrily. 'I told them how Zena and Chantrelle have been leaving me alone lately, and how the gang's kind of split up, and they were really encouraged. They couldn't believe it when I told them that Chantrelle's turned into a swot!'

Frenchy nudged Lulu. 'Yeah, it's pretty amazing,' she agreed.

Lulu couldn't help smiling. Across the courtyard, Zena Lemon kept stepping up onto a low wall, then jumping off, trying very hard to look like someone who felt like being on her own right now, thank you. Lulu almost felt sorry for her; she had so completely lost face at Mrs Pye's little award ceremony, there was nothing left for her to poke fun at others about. Shunned by Chantrelle, and now Cara and Mel too, for no longer being the anti-heroine they had so admired, she cut a truly pathetic figure.

'So my parents have decided to give Ferretsmore another chance,' said Glynnie.

'Well, I think we should celebrate!' said Lulu. 'Hey, it's almost half-term, no school for a week...why don't you both come for a sleepover?'

'Excellent!' enthused Frenchy.

'Oh thanks, Lu,' said Glynnie. 'I'd really love to, but I can't; we're going away.' She stood up. 'Listen, I'll catch you later...gotta tell the others...bye!'

'Wow,' said Frenchy, after Glynnie had gone. 'Amazing, huh?'

'Yeah,' said Lulu, dreamily. 'You know what? I'm quite blown away by this.'

'Well, of course you are!' said Frenchy. 'I mean, it's all thanks to you, isn't it? You deserve a whopping great pat on the back for what you've done, Lu.'

'No, it's more than that,' said Lulu. 'I can't quite put it into words; I feel...*powerful*, I guess. In a really good way. But I couldn't have done it without you, French.

Hey, I hope *you're* coming for that sleepover?'

'Well, we're around, so…yeah!'

'Good,' said Lulu. 'We're not going away till Sunday, so I'm sure it'll be OK.'

Disappearing Apples

Lulu hummed happily to herself as she brought a tray of brownies and juice into her bedroom, then nearly dropped it when she caught sight of Varaminta on her computer screen; Frenchy was watching a webcast of *The Fashion Police*. 'Aargh! What have you got that on for?' Lulu cried, her insides twisting into knots.

'Oh! I just put it on 'cause I thought it would be fun for target practice,' said Frenchy. 'Watch.' She took the piece of gum from her mouth and aimed it at the screen. It landed squarely on Varaminta's behind. 'Ha, excellent shot!' cried Frenchy, jumping up and down. 'OK, your turn!'

Lulu put down the tray, then winced as she grabbed her belly. 'Uh, you know what? I'm starving, let's eat.'

Frenchy shrugged and put the computer to 'sleep' mode. 'Oh, all right then.' She sat down and reached for a brownie.

Lulu realised she needed a moment for the pain to subside before she could eat anything. 'Uh-uh-uh!' she teased, holding the plate out of the way. 'I've...got another idea for a game; you have to *earn* your brownie points by doing whatever I say. How about...I know, do an impression!'

'OK, I've got one,' said Frenchy, standing up. She scowled, slumped her shoulders forward and began stomping around the room, which soon had Lulu rolling around the floor with laughter.

'Oh, that's brilliant!' she cried. She didn't need to say who it was.

They took it in turns doing impressions, each one more outrageous than the last, and were soon in fits of giggles. Finally, exhausted, they collapsed in a heap and finished off the brownies. Frenchy peered up at the stars through Lulu's skylight. 'It's...that one,' she said, pointing. 'Is it?'

Lulu shook her head. 'Uh-uh. It's moved way over to the right...see?' she said, pointing out her Truth Star. 'It's something like the twelfth brightest star, and it's always got those two fainter stars next to it.'

'And you really think it talks to you?' said Frenchy. She started to giggle again. 'Sorry, Lu, I'm just in a silly mood.'

Lulu suppressed a smile. 'I know, it sounds daft. Anyway, no, of course it doesn't literally *talk* to me. It just sort of helps me follow my instincts. I can't really explain how...it just does. I find I can focus my thoughts on it even when it's cloudy now.'

'And...that's Venus over there, right?' said Frenchy. 'That one's easy to spot.'

'Venus, or Hesperus,' Lulu said, reminding Frenchy of the planet's name as the evening star. 'The *Apple* Star. You know, that's why Ambrosia May gave the book that name.'

'Oh yeah, I know, the Apples of the Hesperides,' said Frenchy, remembering the Greek myth Cassandra had talked about, the eleventh labour of Heracles. His task was to steal the golden apples from three nymphs called the Hesperides, after whom Hesperus was named. The task was considered impossible, as the apples were guarded by a hundred-headed snake.

'No, I don't just mean the mythological connection,' said Lulu. 'It goes deeper than that; I realised it after that whole Cupid Cakes episode. The Apple Star is the star of *love*, and love is the reason for everything that's in the book.'

Frenchy frowned. 'How d'you mean?'

Lulu rolled over and propped herself up on her elbows. 'It comes down to why you use the recipes;

you've got to be motivated by love. I don't mean romantic love, I mean caring about people. *Really* caring. I understand now why the recipes don't work in the right way if the book falls into the wrong hands. If you used a recipe for any other reason: fear, hatred, greed...even just plain noseyness, then the magic would be corrupted and result in a bad outcome. That's why things didn't exactly go according to plan with the Cupid Cakes; I was acting more out of fear than anything else.'

'And the Truth Cookies?'

'OK, I admit there was some fear and loathing there too – perhaps that's why there were one or two hitches along the way – but what I did was mostly out of love for Dad.'

'So, the more evil the intent of the user, the more evil the outcome,' said Frenchy.

'Exactly.'

'Blimey. You'd think old Ambrosia Whatsit could've come up with something a bit less risky!'

'Hey, don't be so hard on her!' exclaimed Lulu. 'She did her best. And the way it's fixed so you can't copy it...*that's* a stroke of genius.'

'It's – what?'

'Didn't I tell you? Oh no, you were away. I discovered this over the summer holidays – it's amazing! See, I'd decided I was going to copy out the whole thing – so I had a spare, right? Just in case. So I wrote out the first recipe...and what do you think happened? It just started fading before my eyes! Disappeared completely from the page.'

'You are kidding.'

'No way. So the next thing I did, I tried doing it on the computer, and guess what – the minute I hit "save" – *pfft*! Gone. I tried hitting "print" first – same thing. Here, I'll show you if you don't believe me.' Lulu got up and went over to the shelf above her desk where she kept the cut-out encyclopedia. She pulled it down and opened it. What she saw was such a shock, she let out a squeal of horror. The encyclopedia fell from her hands onto the keyboard, causing the computer to start up again with an ominous groan.

Frenchy jumped up. 'What is it, Lu?'

Lulu stared at her blankly for a moment. Varaminta, back on the computer screen in close-up, was laughing scornfully.

'*The Apple Star*,' Lulu managed at last. 'It's gone.'

Wilted Flowers

'OK, calm down,' said Frenchy, shutting down the computer. She pulled two pieces of bubblegum from her pocket and handed one to Lulu. 'There's got to be a simple explanation for this. Are you *sure* you put it back?'

'Yes, of course I'm sure!' insisted Lulu, flapping her arms. 'O-oh!'

'All right; when was the last time you used it?'

'When I made the brainy things, of course – the, the Nuggets!' stammered Lulu, pacing up and down.

'Hmm,' said Frenchy. 'That was, what – two weeks ago?'

'Uh, nearly, yes.'

'You're *sure* you haven't taken it out at all since then?'

Lulu chewed her gum thoughtfully. 'Yes, I'm absolutely positive. Oh French, it's been stolen! *How* could this have happened?'

'OK, don't panic,' said Frenchy. 'We still haven't eliminated all the most likely explanations.'

'Huh? Like what?'

'Like the possibility that your dad or Aileen might have it.'

'What? Come on, French, neither of them would just *take it away* like that, surely.'

Frenchy adjusted her glasses. 'I think we'd have to find out, before jumping to any other conclusions.'

Lulu dropped heavily onto the bed. 'Do you really think so?'

'Think about it, Lu. You've probably done more cooking these past few weeks than ever before. And what with your secret stash in the attic, and all those weird plants you've got in the garden—'

'Oh my God, the *garden*!' cried Lulu suddenly, standing bolt upright.

'Lu, you look deathly pale – what is it?'

'Last week, there was someone…Andreas. Oh no! I didn't *think*…' Lulu fell silent. Then she turned to Frenchy and explained gravely, 'French, there was a substitute gardener last week.'

'Oh,' said Frenchy darkly.

'And…here's the worst part; I recognised him. At least…I didn't *know* I recognised him at the time, not exactly. I just thought he seemed vaguely familiar – you know, like you do sometimes. But I didn't think anything of it...and then I was getting the Nuggets ready and my head was full of the test, and there was that letter for Aileen—'

'Lu, where had you seen him before?'

'Not *him*, French...*her*. It was Grodmila.'

Frenchy gasped. 'It couldn't have been!'

'Oh yes it could. And remember what Aileen said – that Grodmila's still working for Varaminta? It all fits....oh, how could I have been so stupid? I should have realised; those puffy eyes...they were almost hidden by his – *her* hat. But not completely. Otherwise she looked totally different. All whiskery, so I couldn't see that big ugly mole of hers – that would have been a dead giveaway. It must have been a professional make-up job.'

'And if there's anything Varaminta knows about, it's make-up,' added Frenchy. 'She probably has a whole phone book crammed with make-up artists.'

'But the eyes are the one thing you can't really change,' said Lulu, her stomach turning over now more than ever. 'No, it was her, all right. Same height...same *voice*, now I come to think of it. But how could she have got upstairs to snoop around without Aileen noticing?'

'Maybe she waited for Aileen to go out.'

'Yes, but then Aileen would have locked up. Costas wouldn't have given Grodmila a key – he doesn't have one. He just comes and goes by the side door to the garden... Oh no, I've just thought of something; Grodmila would have known about the drawer where the spare key is kept! She was probably able to sneak into the kitchen and get it while Aileen was upstairs.'

'You should check then; see if the spare key is still there. Go on, have a look; I'm going to stay here and think some more.'

Lulu's mind was racing as she made her way downstairs. So *this* was why she'd been getting those strange belly-churnings every time she saw Varaminta! She should have trusted her gut instinct, and realised it was a warning...instead she had ignored it, thinking she was just being neurotic. Meanwhile she had allowed herself to be lulled into a false sense of security concerning Varaminta and Torquil because they had stopped hounding her for *The Apple Star*. And she had been so convinced that Varaminta had moved on since becoming a media celebrity. But Lulu had fallen into a trap; that was exactly what she had been supposed to think! And as a result she had completely overlooked the magical security rituals she had learned from Cassandra. There had been little flowers Lulu had planted...now withered with neglect since she had become more interested in her other plants. And there had been a little bottle of special fluid for sprinkling around the house…Lulu wasn't even sure where that was now.

'The key's still there,' she told Frenchy when she returned.

'No, the key's there *again*,' said Frenchy. 'I've been thinking, and I half expected you to say that; it makes sense. Grodmila wouldn't want to rouse suspicion, so after she got The Apple Star, she probably locked the back door from the inside and replaced the key. Then she probably climbed out through a window or something.'

Lulu went over to her skylight. 'Oh boy. This isn't closed properly.'

'There you go.'

'But it's on the roof!' protested Lulu, still reeling in disbelief. 'Surely—'

'She'd have been prepared for that,' said Frenchy. 'And it's at the back of the house.'

Lulu thought for a moment. 'Well then, we've been burgled! I'll tell Dad I've had something stolen – it could be anything – and then he can report it. Get on to Costas and track her down.'

'Lu, who do you think you're kidding? You think all it takes is for Costas to call Grodmila? No way!

Whatever phone number he'd have had for this fake Andros or whatever, it's not going to work now! And there's no way he'd have an address. Face it, Lu; we're just going to have to work out how to get that book back ourselves.'

Red Sweet Treat

Lulu had never had a sleepover that didn't end up with staying up and chatting well into the night. 'Sleepover' was really the wrong word; 'talkathon' was more like it. And this was the talkathon to end them all.

Lulu found the feeling of loss quite overwhelming. It felt as if someone had come along and cut a great chunk out of her, and it wasn't until now that she realised just how much *The Apple Star* and her mum had become fused together in her imagination. Even though she couldn't be sure that the handwritten inscription in the book, addressed to 'Lulu' and signed 'Mum', was really from her, it nevertheless felt almost like losing Mum all over again.

'Oh good grief, French,' said Lulu heavily. 'Dad and I are leaving for the country tomorrow!'

'Don't worry,' said Frenchy. 'It's only for three nights, right? And this needs careful planning anyway, so it's not as if we'd be able to get *The Apple Star* back straightaway.'

Lulu realised this was true, but all the same the anxiety was eating away at her. She paced about the room, wringing her hands. 'But what if she...? I mean, she might...'

'Look, we can't drive ourselves crazy thinking about what might happen before we get the book back,' Frenchy reasoned. 'We just have to concentrate on our plan. OK, we're both agreed that trying to break into Varaminta's house would be too dangerous.'

'Right,' said Lulu. 'And anyway, Varaminta's bound to have it safely under lock and key. All the same, we should get hold of her address.'

'Jot that down, then,' suggested Frenchy; they were compiling a list of things they could do.

Lulu stopped pacing and took up her pen. 'Boy, French, if only you had a mobile phone, we'd at least be able to discuss this while I'm away.'

'I'm saving up for one,' said Frenchy. 'Look, concentrate! What's Varaminta going to do about getting ingredients?'

Lulu threw the pen down. 'I've *got* to talk to Cassandra!' She picked up her phone and rang her, but her heart sank when yet again she got the voicemail message. 'Cassandra, something *awful* has happened,' she said in a low, trembling voice. 'Please call me as soon as possible, I'm very worried!' She hung up, remembering with dismay how Cassandra could sometimes be unreachable for weeks at a time. 'Oh French, she could be away in Cairo or something; she might be gone for weeks!'

'Mmm,' said Frenchy thoughtfully. 'I wonder if it's no coincidence.'

'What do you mean?'

'That man who came after us at Cassandra's house – maybe there's some connection between him and Varaminta. Perhaps she had him follow us there?'

Lulu frowned. 'No. Don't you remember how Cassandra said it definitely wasn't someone who was after me? "I know exactly who it is," she said. "Someone who thinks they can take everything away from me."'

'You're right,' admitted Frenchy. 'Besides, if it had been anything to do with you or *The Apple Star*, Cassandra would have done everything she could to warn you of the danger, and advise you what to do.'

'Exactly,' said Lulu. She sighed. 'But I still keep thinking about that day; I can't help feeling something bad must have happened to her, even though she laughed it off as if that sort of thing happens all the time.'

'Perhaps it does,' said Frenchy. 'I guess it must do, or she'd hardly go to the trouble of having all those secret walls and everything.'

'Well, for whatever reason, we know she didn't get my first phone message or the letter I sent her,' Lulu pointed out. 'If she had, she definitely would have been in touch.'

'You're right there,' agreed Frenchy. 'All right, what else can we do?'

*

It was nearly two o'clock in the morning by the time they fell asleep, and they didn't stir until ten the next morning. After Frenchy had gone, Lulu had to pack for her three-day trip with Dad. Wearily she threw a few things into her bag, but her mind was elsewhere. At some point last night, she and Frenchy had discussed the idea of using Lulu's 'emergency' recipes somehow, but they'd been too exhausted to figure out exactly what they would do with them. Psychic Psours, Medium Sweets, Hush Brownies...

'Lulu?' said Dad, popping his head around the door. 'We're off in twenty minutes...make sure you're all packed, love.'

'Oh, right,' said Lulu, trying not to sound too depressed.

'I'm just going to drop a key in next door,' said Dad.

'OK.' Lulu waited until he was gone, then went up to the attic and opened her wardrobe full of goodies. At least that was untouched. Here was the box of Hush Brownies, and the jars of Psychic Psours and Medium Sweets, all present and correct. She picked up the jar of luscious red sweets. 'Torquil,' she whispered to herself – the Torment. How wonderful it would be to outwit him once again; he had tormented her so much when he had been trying to blackmail her into giving up *The Apple Star*. And the beauty of using the sweets on him was that there would be no battle, since he wouldn't even know what was happening. Of course, it was possible that even if she succeeded in listening in on his thoughts, there wouldn't be anything worth hearing. Lulu shuddered as she imagined for a moment just what it was like inside Torquil's brain. But since there was absolutely no possibility of getting Varaminta to eat them, her trickster son just might provide some vital clues as to how to get *The Apple Star* back; he was the next best chance they had. A treat for the trickster...

'That's it!' said Lulu aloud. Trick or treat; Halloween was just five days away; they would be back by then. Lulu still wasn't quite sure how she would manage it, but Halloween, and the opportunity it presented to spend plenty of time out and about at night, disguised with masks, just had to be the perfect chance to launch their investigation.

If it's not too late, Lulu thought gloomily.

Tiger Prawn

'Lu, I've been dying to talk to you!' came Frenchy's breathless voice down the phone.

Lulu hurried up the stairs while Dad opened his mail in the hallway. She hadn't even taken her coat off after arriving back from the trip, she had been so anxious to speak to Frenchy. 'Me too...look, I still haven't heard a peep out of you-know-who.'

'Cassandra?'

'Mm-hm.'

'Oh, that's too bad,' said Frenchy. 'Well anyway, I've been doing a bit of investigating, and I've got some useful information.'

Lulu hurried into her room and closed the door behind her. 'Really? What is it?'

'OK,' said Frenchy. 'You know your idea about giving Torquil the Medium Sweets?' Lulu had quickly called her about this on Sunday before she left. 'Well, there's this neighbour of mine called Euan – he goes to school with Torquil.'

'Oh yeah, I'd forgotten about him,' said Lulu.

'I was just chatting to him about Halloween,' Frenchy went on, 'and guess what? He and a gang are going trick or treating and I found out that Torquil's going too. But they're not going out 'till at least seven o'clock because Torquil likes to be at home in the early evening to scare the "littlies", as he calls them, when they come to his house.'

'Oh, well done, French – hey, isn't that just *so* like him?'

'Yup,' agreed Frenchy. 'But it's good, isn't it? It means we can pay Torquil a trick-or-treat visit in our Halloween disguises before seven.'

'Right, and give him the Medium Sweets,' added Lulu. 'Kind of the wrong way round, I know, but that's OK. The thing is, we'd need to make sure he ate them straight away...how do we do that?'

'I know, we need to think a bit more about that part,' said Frenchy. 'And we also have to see to it that he doesn't give any away.'

'Well, *that* shouldn't be too hard, knowing Torquil,' said Lulu. 'Still, we can't be too careful. Hmm...'

'Noodle?' called Dad from downstairs. 'Come on, we're waiting for you!'

'Oops!' said Lulu to Frenchy. 'Listen, I'd better go; they must think I'm terribly rude – I'm coming! – Aileen's done some special meal, and I've barely even said hello.'

'Go,' said Frenchy. 'We'll speak tomorrow!'

Lulu tried to sort it all out in her mind as she headed slowly downstairs. It felt like progress, yet she was still very anxious about Cassandra...she still had no idea what they could do about her.

Aileen had indeed prepared them a nice surprise; when Lulu came into the kitchen she had just finished lighting candles and was pouring Dad a glass of wine. 'Hey, Lu – come! Sit down and eat.'

'Wow, Aileen, what a treat!' enthused Dad. He took a bite out of a gigantic tiger prawn. 'Mmm, delicious!'

'Glad you like it!' said Aileen. 'How about you, Lu?'

'It's lovely,' agreed Lulu. 'But then, you always make lovely food.' So do I, she thought, sadly – though not any more.

'Well, this is kind of a thank-you for putting me up,' said Aileen. 'I'll be out of your hair soon – I think I've found a flat at last.'

Dad smoothed his hair back, as if reminded of his newly luxuriant locks by Aileen's remark. 'Oh, right – well, you must be, uh, pleased...' Lulu heard the disappointment in his voice; he'll be even more disappointed when she quits altogether, she thought miserably.

'...But really Aileen, you don't owe us a thing,' Dad was saying. 'We've lov...really liked having you stay...ahem, especially *Lulu*, I mean for *Lulu* it's great – you know, a bit like having a big sister or a...' Hesitating as the word 'mother' dangled in the air, he tried to cover it up by being all jocular. 'Hey, with cooking like this, Aileen, we might not *let* you go, ha ha – eh, Noodle?'

'Mmm,' said Lulu flatly.

Dad looked at her. 'Is anything wrong?'

'No,' said Lulu, forcing herself to smile.

'You sure, kiddo?' said Aileen.

'She's been awfully quiet the last couple of days,' said Dad. 'Lulu? Did you want Aileen to stay longer, is that it?'

'No, really Dad, I'm cool. I've just got a bit of a headache, that's all,' she lied.

'Oh, Aileen, before I forget, there's a letter for you, did you see it?'

Aileen put her fork down and turned bright pink. 'Really? N-no, I didn't see it. Where is it?'

'I came across it just now as I was opening my mail; I left it on the hall table for you,' said Dad. Then, noticing Aileen's agitation, he added, 'Don't worry,

I didn't open this one…and I didn't *read* that other one. It was a mistake, I promise.'

'Oh, I know, it's not that…I'm sorry guys, do you mind if I just go take a look?' Aileen dabbed her mouth with her napkin and got up.

'Go ahead,' urged Dad.

Lulu's heart missed a beat. The job application! Seconds later, a strange sound came from the hallway, a sort of yelp.

Dad scraped his seat back. 'Aileen, you OK?'

There was no response for a moment. Then Aileen reappeared, the opened letter in her hand. Her eyes stared blankly in an expression of amazement.

Dad got up and moved towards her. 'Hey, have you had some bad news?'

'No!' said Aileen quickly. 'No, not at all…no worries.' She stuffed the letter into her pocket and sat back down at the table. 'So!' she said brightly. 'How's the food?'

'*Aileen!*' cried Lulu. 'What is it? What was in the letter?'

Aileen paused, then shrugged. 'Oh, it's…just something I've won, that's all.'

Lulu filled with dread.

'Don't tell me you've won a million in the lottery?' said Dad.

'No...'

Lulu waited. Come on, out with it.

'...Not the lottery, and not a million, I'm afraid. Just a small prize draw; less than a hundred,' concluded Aileen eventually, beaming now.

'Oh well, that's cause enough for celebration, I'd say,' said Dad, raising his wine glass. 'Congratulations!'

Lulu was dumbfounded; she didn't know what to think. Was Aileen covering up about the teaching job? And if so, why?

'Lulu?' said Dad, still holding up his glass.

'Oh, yes,' said Lulu at last, raising her water glass. 'Congratulations.'

*

After dinner, Lulu unpacked her things, then spent some time jotting down notes to herself about the Halloween plan. She carefully thought over every minute of it; nothing must go wrong.

Once again, her thoughts were interrupted by Dad calling from downstairs. 'Lulu, phone for you!' he yelled.

Surprised, Lulu looked at her watch; it was already nearly ten o'clock. 'Coming!' she called.

It was Frenchy again. 'Lu, I've just seen something totally freaky in Monday's newspaper,' she whispered.

'What is it?'

'Oh no, Mum's saying I have to get off the phone. Listen, I've rescued the paper from the recycling pile...you're coming round tomorrow, right? I'll show it to you then.'

'But French—'

'Look I've really got to go, Mum's *insisting* she needs the phone right now...bye!'

Oh good grief! thought Lulu. What on earth was this 'freaky' thing? Not for the first time, Lulu found herself cursing Frenchy for not having a mobile phone. She went on a hunt for a copy of Monday's paper but had no luck; she even tried calling Frenchy back, but the line remained engaged until very late. Lulu gave up; she would have to wait until tomorrow to find out what it was.

The Star Ingredient

'Come on then, let's see it!' urged Lulu impatiently, the moment they were safely enclosed out of earshot in Frenchy's bedroom.

Frenchy pulled the newspaper clipping from a drawer. 'Here,' she said, and thrust it into Lulu's grasping hands.

At first she didn't understand what Frenchy was getting at; it was an advertisement for *The Fashion Police*, similar to others that had been appearing since before the series began. This one featured a head-and-shoulders picture of Varaminta in her 'police' gear, and in the bottom right corner it said *The Fashion Police*, with the programme information below.

But as soon as Lulu read the main part of the ad, she knew exactly what Frenchy was so worked up about. It read:

Lulu gasped. The message could not have been more obvious: I have *The Apple Star* but I don't know where to get the ingredients; get in touch if you can help. 'Well, that proves it,' she said, as soon as she could collect her thoughts. 'If there was ever any doubt that the book was stolen on Varaminta's behalf, there certainly isn't now. And you say this went out on Monday?'

'That's right.'

'She might have had some response by now...although I must admit, I find it hard to imagine there's another Cassandra out there – least of all, one who would respond to this kind of thing. You really think there might be? And that they'd know what *The Apple Star* is?'

'I don't think you can assume Cassandra's the only one,' said Frenchy. 'And if there is someone else, I reckon they'd be *very* likely to have heard of *The Apple Star*.'

Lulu stared at the ad, shaking her head slowly in amazement. 'What's "plebeian", anyway?'

'Oh, I looked that up – it's just the sort of word you'd expect a snob like Varaminta to use; it means low-class.'

Lulu thought for a moment. 'Hey, what if we called that number ourselves? I mean, with a fake voice, or something...pretend we've got the ingredients, then lead her on some wild goose chase to – I don't know, an empty warehouse or something – then trap her and bingo! We get *The Apple Star* back.'

Frenchy raised her eyebrows. 'Lu! That's a bit cloak-and-dagger, don't you think?'

Lulu put her hands on her hips indignantly. 'Well, why not?'

'We-ell,' said Frenchy. 'For one thing, we'd have to call from a phone box.'

'A what?'

'You know, those booths in the street...really, Lu! You can't just call from your own phone, you know; Varaminta might be able to trace calls.'

'Oh.'

'*Plus* we'd need to think of an address to give...*and* we'd need help. Come on, Lu, you can't seriously imagine we'd be able to trap her by ourselves! Besides, who would we get to help us?'

Lulu held her hands up. 'OK, OK, I admit, I hadn't really thought it all out.' She sighed. 'Too bad I wasn't able to make some Mighty Muffins as an "emergency" recipe.'

'Oh yeah,' agreed Frenchy. 'I guess they'd have gone all mouldy.'

'That would have been brilliant,' said Lulu, drifting off into a daydream. She imagined herself and Frenchy, going after Varaminta and Torquil in their Halloween disguises, having beefed up their strength to Herculean dimensions with the Mighty Muffins, vanquishing the enemy in true superhero style.

Thinking about the recipe she couldn't make just made Lulu even more painfully aware of the hopelessness of the situation. Their little plan with the Psychic Psours and Medium Sweets seemed pathetically inadequate. The awfulness of it all was more cruelly brought home to her than ever by that superior, mocking face of Varaminta le Bone gazing out of the newspaper clipping. To think that this *woman* should have her wonderful book, the one inscribed, For my lovely Lulu, and signed Mum, was such an obscene distortion of justice, it made Lulu feel sick.

'French, say it one more time, so I can believe it?' she said, her eyes filling with tears. 'Tell me we'll get it back.'

'We will, Lu; I promise.'

*

That evening, Lulu sat gloomily in her room, staring at her Mum-in-Muddy-Wellies picture. She thought about a conversation she'd once had with Frenchy, about the three nymphs called the Hesperides that Ambrosia May talked about in *The Apple Star*, and how she, as owner of the book, was one of the few people to 'reach into that world and learn its secrets'.

'Is Ambrosia May saying those three nymphs actually existed?' Frenchy had asked. 'Like they're your ancestors or something?'

Lulu had said that she'd wondered the same thing, and decided it might just be true. 'I mean not *literally*.' she had said. 'It's a myth, of course. But perhaps there were once three women who lived in some magical garden and held the secrets of *The Apple Star*, and

131

maybe I'm one of their descendants.'

'Which would mean your mum was, too,' Frenchy had said.

Those words went around in Lulu's head as she gazed at Mum's picture now; once again she felt consumed with a sense of loss.

There was a knock at the door; it was Dad. 'Noodle, I've just been having a chat with Aileen,' he said. 'Can you come downstairs for a moment?'

Oh boy, here we go, thought Lulu as she got up to join him. There was something about the way Dad tended to use the term 'having a chat'; it always seemed to mean bad news.

*

'...So you see, this really is a fantastic opportunity,' Aileen said, as she rounded off her whole explanation about how she had been offered the trainee teaching job.

Lulu stared blankly in front of her. 'Was that the letter you got yesterday then?' she asked.

'Well, yeah...but I was sure there would be loads of applicants; I never really thought I'd get the job, to be honest. So when I got the letter I was completely gobsmacked...'

'I could tell that!' said Dad.

'...And I needed time for it to sink in, so I could figure out what to do. In fact, half of me just wanted to forget all about it. That's why I didn't tell you right away what it really was.'

There was silence for a moment. 'Well...you *should* go for it,' said Dad at last. He sighed, and ran his fingers through his hair. 'Although Lulu and I...uh, really don't want to lose you.' Lulu thought she heard his voice crack a little. He stood up and began pacing around. 'But...you're young! You're intelligent, capable; I'm sure you had just that star ingredient they were looking for...' What an unfortunate choice of words, thought Lulu, wryly. And did he really have to go so overboard in his effort to sound as if he was pleased for Aileen? 'This is a fantastic opportunity,' he went on in his excessively enthusiastic way, 'you'd be *mad* not to take it—'

At this, Aileen broke down in tears. 'Oh Michael, you don't know what a hard decision this has been for me!' she cried. 'Please don't think I haven't loved every minute of working for yoo-hoo-hooo!' She took out a tissue and sobbed into it.

This was too much for Lulu, and she was soon in tears as well. Aileen put her arms around her and they had a good old blub together. Lulu was vaguely aware of Dad standing around awkwardly for a moment, before diving out of the room and leaving them to it.

This is all my fault, thought Lulu; it would never have happened without my stupid Chocolate Wishes! Right now, making those for Aileen seemed like the worst decision she could possibly have made. To hell with doing what's best for others! she thought. What about *me*?! Dad was right; Aileen was more like a big sister than a housekeeper – no, like a favourite aunt. And now she was leaving.

I must have been out of my mind, she told herself.

Halloween Message

At last the big day came: Halloween.

As Lulu and Frenchy arrived at Lulu's house after school, Aileen announced that she had a surprise. 'Ta-da! Whaddaya think, Lu?' she said, holding up a costume.

'Hey, that's great!' said Frenchy.

'D'you like it? I designed it myself, of course!'

Lulu took the costume and held it up against her. It was a zombie outfit, a Victorian-style dress complete with fake bloodstains on it and shreds of ripped muslin trailing from it. 'Wow, it looks like something out of a movie!' she said. 'It's dead clever.'

'Yeah, it's *dead* clever all right!' laughed Aileen. 'I figured you needed something to go with your zombie mask. And look, it's got a nice deep pocket for you to store your goodies in. Well, gotta get on with supper; go and put it on so I can see you in it!'

'Yeah, I will,' said Lulu. 'Thanks Aileen, it's really

brilliant!' She took the costume and went upstairs with Frenchy.

'I hope you're going to be OK in that long skirt,' said Frenchy, as soon as they got to Lulu's room. 'You know, if you've got a lot of running to do or something.'

'Mmm,' said Lulu. 'So do I...that was so nice of her to make it though, wasn't it?'

'Of course,' said Frenchy. 'See, she really cares about you, Lu; that won't change.' Lulu had told Frenchy all about how Aileen had decided to take a new career path and become a teacher. 'You'll still see her – hey, you should be thankful she's not going back to Australia!'

'I know,' admitted Lulu. 'It just won't be the same, that's all.' She consulted her watch. 'Right, we have an hour and a half to get ready, eat and get out of here. You've got your outfit, right?'

'Of course!' said Frenchy, unloading her Frankenstein gear and mask from her backpack. The masks were essential as disguise for when they were to visit Torquil. 'OK,' she added, adjusting her glasses. 'Let's go over this one more time: we *bring* the Hush Brownies with us, but don't eat them right away...'

'That's right,' said Lulu, pulling out her checklist. 'Even though they don't silence the voice, I don't want there to be anything unusual about us when we visit Torquil, that could make him suspicious.'

'...And *I'm* the one who eats the Psychic Psours,' Frenchy continued, 'so that you can concentrate on picking up signals from your Truth Star—'

'If any!' Lulu seriously doubted she was capable of picking up detailed enough instructions from her guiding star to help them in their current predicament. But she decided she might as well try. 'And don't forget,' she added, '*you* do all the talking when we go to Torquil's. He mustn't hear my voice, or he might recognise it.'

Frenchy nodded. 'OK, now, I've been thinking about how we make sure he eats the Medium Sweets right away and doesn't share them. This is absolutely crucial – most likely, he'll have a friend or two with him, and the whole thing will be a mess if more than one of them eats them.'

'Oh boy, you're telling me!' agreed Lulu, as she climbed into her zombie frock. 'I feel sorry for you as it is; just going inside Torquil's brain and being assaulted by all those nasty thoughts is bad enough. But jumbled up with someone else's as well – it could drive you crazy!'

'Exactly. But as you pointed out, he's greedy, so the not-sharing part shouldn't be too hard. And I've had an idea; I was inspired by those Chocolate Wishes you made for Aileen. Will it be enough if he has three of the sweets?'

'Oh, like three wishes, you mean?' said Lulu, pulling the dress over her shoulders. 'Yes, I think so – although I can't check the recipe because...' she trailed off, despondently.

'All right; he'll definitely want all three wishes for himself, even if he's not convinced,' said Frenchy. 'And we tell him he's *got* to eat them on Halloween, or the wishes won't come true.'

'What if he doesn't eat them for four or five hours?'

Frenchy raised an eyebrow in an expression of ridicule. 'Are you kidding? He'll eat them right away, guaranteed. OK, next thing is, we have to get over to Hackney...boy, we're going to be gone some time, aren't we?'

'Yeah, but Dad's cool,' said Lulu. 'As far as he's concerned we're going to a party, and we're getting a lift back. I'll have my phone, so if we end up being really late, I can always make up some sort of story.'

Lulu slipped her phone into the pocket of the dress; Frenchy would carry everything else in her backpack. When they had finished dressing, they headed up to the attic to get the Psychic Psours, Medium Sweets and the Hush Brownies. They put them in the backpack, with some spare Sweets and Psours in Lulu's pocket, just in case.

As they came back down from the attic, Frenchy peered out through a small window that looked out onto an area of flat roof. She paused. 'What's that cat doing there?'

'Huh?' Lulu looked out. The cat stared back intently, and miaowed at her. Suddenly, Lulu was filled with a sense of dread. 'Oh French! That's not just any old cat...that's *Cassandra's* cat!'

Frenchy gasped. 'Oh boy, you're right...Rameses.'

Lulu's hands trembled as she opened the window to let in the familiar sleek brown cat, so unlike any other she'd ever seen. 'Oh no,' she breathed. 'Cassandra's in trouble...I knew it!'

Rameses jumped inside, his collar tinkling as he did so. He purred loudly as he stood on the stair in front of her, rubbing vigorously against her muslin skirts. 'Look – he's got something round his neck.' Lulu shut the window and bent down to take a closer look at the cat's collar, which had a locket about the size of a pencil sharpener attached to it. On it was a picture of an eye.

Frenchy kneeled beside her. 'That's an Egyptian Wadjet Eye...for warding off evil.'

Lulu turned it over and saw there was a tiny clasp

at the side. She lifted it, and the locket opened up. Rameses stared at her with his startling silver-blue eyes as she did so. 'There's something inside!' Lulu took out the tiny piece of paper, folded into a neat little concertina, opened it out and read its message:

IF THIS HAS REACHED YOU, IT MEANS I AM IN DANGER — PROBABLY FROM MY COUSIN, OMAR RISHNEP. FIND HIM AND YOU WILL FIND ME. CASSANDRA.

Medium Sweets

'Omar,' breathed Lulu, the word forming a wisp of white vapour in the cold evening air. Her appetite quite thoroughly banished, she had merely picked at the dinner Aileen had prepared. Now they were at last venturing out, following Rameses to they knew not where. Being found by him had suddenly changed everything; getting *The Apple Star* back could wait. Finding Cassandra was all that mattered.

'Omar,' echoed Frenchy. 'The one who ridiculed Cassandra's prediction. "The wind blew through her ears."'

'It must have been him that day, French,' said Lulu. 'That man who tried to chase after us.'

'Or an accomplice of his – and those men in the van who followed us from school…they must be connected to him as well,' added Frenchy. 'I guess you were right after all. Perhaps Cassandra managed to shake him off that time, but he came back. The question is, *why?*'

Suddenly she stopped in her tracks, making Lulu stop too. Rameses stood and stared up at them expectantly. 'OK, we seriously need to figure out what we're doing here.'

'What do you mean?' asked Lulu, puzzled. 'We're following Rameses.'

'Lu, how long do you suppose it took him to find you? You tried phoning Cassandra when – Saturday, right?'

'Right.'

'Lu, it's now Friday…for all we know, it might have taken Rameses a week or more to get here. Are we really just going to walk and walk endlessly, following a cat?'

'Well, put that way, I guess it does sound a bit daft,' admitted Lulu.

'Not to mention *slow*,' added Frenchy. 'Plus, has it occurred to you that there could be a link between what's happened to Cassandra, and Varaminta's advertisement for ingredients for *The Apple Star*?'

'But like you said, I was getting no response from Cassandra on Saturday,' Lulu pointed out. 'The ad didn't appear until Monday.'

'True…all the same, I think we should still go to Torquil's. It won't take long, and who knows what we might find out? We won't have another chance to pay him a trick-or-treat visit for a whole year.'

'All right,' said Lulu. 'And we keep Rameses with us.'

'Of course,' said Frenchy. 'Come on.'

*

They spotted the house some way off; it was the only one on the street almost entirely transformed by Halloween garb. While his neighbours contented themselves with the odd pumpkin jack-o'-lantern or two outside, Torquil had sprayed fake cobwebs everywhere he could reach. The front garden had been transformed into a gothic graveyard, and there was even dry ice belching out from somewhere near the front door, which some small Halloween-costumed children were approaching with glee.

'Impressive,' Frenchy admitted, her voice sounding hollow from behind her Frankenstein mask.

'Yes,' said Lulu, as the front door opened. 'But if I know Torquil, underneath it all is something a whole lot nastier.'

As if on cue, one of the children, a little boy dressed as Spiderman, let out a bloodcurdling scream. This set off his companions, and they all raced back down the garden path, spangly capes flying, to the worried-looking mother waiting at the garden gate.

'See what I mean?' said Lulu.

'EEYAA-YAAA-WAAH!!' howled the smallest child, leaping into its mother's arms, while the young Spiderman cried, 'It was all slimy, Mummy!' and the rest of them cowered behind her.

'*You ought to be ashamed of yourself!*' shrieked the mother at Torquil.

'What?' replied Torquil from the doorway, feigning innocence. 'They gave me the choice of "trick or treat", so I gave them the trick. If they only wanted a treat, they should've said!'

'That's *not* how it works, and you know it!' yelled the mother, struggling to make herself heard over the din of the traumatised children.

'Suit yerself!' said Torquil, and he shut the door.

The woman marched up the road with her charges towards Lulu and Frenchy. 'Don't go to *that* house!' she warned.

'It was all *slimy*, Mummy!' repeated Spiderman.

'What happened?' asked Lulu.

'He offered them a bag of what *should* have been sweets,' said the woman. 'But—'

'It was all slimy!' cried Spiderman again. 'Like...slugs! I think it was slugs, Mummy!'

'Never mind, darling, we won't go to that nasty place ever again,' said Mummy, and off they went.

Frenchy handed Lulu three Medium Sweets from

her backpack, and they ventured towards the house. Rameses slowed down to a halt, emitting the same hostile rumblings as he had done when Cassandra's unwelcome visitor arrived.

'That cat certainly is a good judge of character,' remarked Lulu.

'Let him stay here,' said Frenchy, as Rameses arched his back and bristled his fur. 'He'll wait for us.'

Dry ice practically engulfed them as they approached the house. The front door was now ajar, and from behind it came sound effects of whistling wind and creaking hinges. Lulu felt slightly sick at the prospect of coming face to face with Torquil again, and her nausea was only made worse by the acrid dry ice and the sweaty rubber smell from inside her zombie mask. But she pressed on and rang the doorbell. The door fell open to reveal a 'corpse' lying in a pool of fake blood, apparently with an arm severed and an eyeball dangling. A new addition to the montage, it seemed; Torquil was certainly going to town with the horror theme. Then Torquil himself appeared suddenly from behind the door, making both girls jump.

Don't be put off, Lulu kept telling herself, as she observed him through her mask-holes. He was dressed as Count Dracula. An evil bloodsucker; how well the guise suited him!

'Well?' he said.

'Trick or treat!' Frenchy chimed loudly.

Torquil peered around them. 'What, haven't you got any littlies with you?'

'No...we do a different kind of Halloween visit,' said Frenchy, affecting a deep voice that Lulu could tell was an effort to sound all mystical and Cassandra-like. Frenchy took a step forward. 'We give out treats...*special* ones!' she added. The whirling wind sounds added superbly to the magical effect she was striving for.

Lulu suppressed a nervous giggle.

Torquil regarded them sideways. 'What sort of special ones?'

Lulu held out her hand with the three luscious, shiny Medium Sweets.

'Three wishes!' Frenchy went on. 'Make one wish for each sweet...but don't leave it too late, because...' She coughed, the dry ice apparently taking its toll. '...because...' She coughed again, harder this time.

Torquil sneered. 'Because what?' he asked, glancing at Lulu as if expecting her to take over.

Lulu remained mute, desperate not to speak in case Torquil were to recognise her voice. Oh come on, French! she thought, willing her to get over her coughing fit.

'Ahem, because the sweets *must* be eaten on

Halloween,' said Frenchy at last, 'or else the wishes won't work!'

Lulu held her hand up higher, bringing the rosy-red sweets closer to Torquil's nose.

Torquil eyed her; Lulu felt as if he could see right through her mask. 'Ha!' he sneered. 'What a load of old codswallop!'

'I'll have 'em then,' came a voice from behind him, as the 'corpse' sat up, forgetting his role.

'No, you won't!' snapped Torquil as he grabbed the sweets. 'They're mine!'

'But don't forget,' said Frenchy, 'you must eat them tonight!'

'Yeah, yeah,' said Torquil, slipping the sweets into the pocket of his Dracula trousers. Then he reached behind him and brought forward a small plastic bag. 'And now it's time for *your* treat!' he announced, smirking.

'No thanks,' said Frenchy quickly. She nudged Lulu. 'Come on.'

'Tuh! Too bad,' said Torquil, as Lulu and Frenchy turned to leave.

A split second later, Lulu felt the ground shift beneath her, and both she and Frenchy were thrown off balance and tumbled head over heels down three steps, onto the garden path.

'Ha ha ha!' Torquil was doubled up with laughter at the spectacle.

Immediately she was on the ground, Lulu realised two things: firstly, that the cause of their fall was the strip of Astroturf beneath them, which they had not seen under all the dry ice, and which Torquil had apparently yanked at to dislodge them; and secondly, that her zombie mask had gone seriously askew. She desperately tried to straighten it, while simultaneously struggling to her feet in her voluminous muslin trailing skirts. Holding the dress up with one hand, the mask in place with the other, she hobbled back down the garden path, following Frenchy, who Lulu was glad to see was apparently unhurt. The creaky-hinge-whistling-wind sound effects mingled with Torquil's malicious laughter as they retreated.

Psychic Psours

Lulu and Frenchy kept going, maintaining as much dignity as they could muster, until they reached the end of the block and rounded the corner. Then, heaving huge sighs of relief, they removed their masks and leaned on a garden wall until they got their breath back. Rameses trotted eagerly up to them.

Lulu winced, clutching her leg. 'Ow, ow, ow!'

'Oh, Lu, are you OK?' said Frenchy.

'Uh...yeah, I'll be all right. I just bashed my shin, that's all.'

'And I've banged my elbow,' said Frenchy, stuffing the masks into her backpack. 'Blimey, he doesn't get any nicer with age, does he?'

'Nope...oh French, I'm just so glad he didn't see my face – well, not enough of it, anyway. I nearly lost my mask!'

'Don't worry,' said Frenchy. 'He couldn't have seen much, not with all that dry ice everywhere.'

'Phew,' said Lulu. 'Well, I guess it didn't go too badly...considering. Now it's time for you to have your Psychic Psours. You should take three, to be in line with the Medium Sweets.'

Frenchy duly pulled the green sweets out of her backpack. 'OK, here goes!' she said, popping one in her mouth. 'Eeee!' she went. 'Sssss! Man, that is *sour*!' Her lips puckered and her cheeks hollowed as she tried to get accustomed to the flavour. 'I have to eat three of these?'

'Sorry,' said Lulu. 'I'd do it myself, but—'

'No, no,' insisted Frenchy. 'It's OK, I can handle it...bleee!'

'They *have* to be really sour, to balance out the sweetness of the Medium Sweets,' explained Lulu. 'It's all to do with Yin and Yang...Cassandra explained it to me. Oh French, I feel terrible...she might have been captured or whatever as much as a week ago, and I did nothing!'

'Lu, you didn't *know*. She told you everything was fine, remember?'

'I know, but I still feel as if I should have realised, when she said that about the "someone" who wanted to "take everything away" from her.'

Frenchy linked arms with her. 'Lu, don't be so hard on yourself. Anyway,' she added, nodding at Rameses, 'we're doing something now.'

Lulu sighed nervously, as she gazed at Rameses. 'I only hope we're not too late.'

*

After following Rameses a little way, Lulu and Frenchy determined that he was definitely intent on heading east. They guessed he was leading them back to Hackney so, to save time, they picked him up and took the bus. 'Here, have a Hush Brownie,' said Lulu, passing one to Frenchy as soon as they were settled in their seats.

'Thanks. Hey, got a spare piece for the cat?' Rameses was sniffing curiously at the brownie.

'Well, I never heard of a cat eating a brownie,' said Lulu, 'but this one looks as if he's ready to eat just about anything, poor thing. Here, puss puss!' Rameses sniffed closer, then started licking the piece she was offering him. Looking at his locket, she added, 'Guess I'll take this off, so it doesn't jangle—'

'*Whoah!*' cried Frenchy suddenly, grabbing Lulu by the arm and leaping out of her seat.

'MIAOOW!!' shrieked Rameses, jumping down from Lulu's lap.

Startled, Lulu dropped the bag of brownies on the floor. 'French! What is it?'

Frenchy held her head in her hands. 'Oh my God, it's happening…Torquil's messing with my brain!'

Lulu turned bright red and glanced furtively around the bus. An old lady seated opposite stared back, her large-framed spectacles giving her the appearance of a disapproving owl. Lulu tried to laugh it off, as she reached down to retrieve the brownies, fortunately still in their bag. Rameses stared wide-eyed at her from under the seat in front. 'It's OK, puss!' whispered Lulu, reaching out in an attempt to quell his alarm. 'Here, *ki ki ki*!' Eventually Rameses came forward and Lulu soon had him back in her lap.

Frenchy, however, sat rigidly upright, her features now locked into a sort of Halloween horror grimace. 'Are you all right?' Lulu whispered.

Frenchy nodded, although she still looked as if she had just tasted something awful. 'Yuh…I'm good. I – I can handle it,' she murmured unconvincingly.

Lulu leaned closer. 'Can you…tell me what you're getting?'

Frenchy's face slackened, and her brow furrowed as she tried to concentrate. 'OK, uh…he's saying…oh man!'

'What? Tell me!'

'SORRY,' Frenchy shouted, like someone trying to make herself heard over loud music, 'IT'S JUST THAT EVERY TIME I…HANG ON…'

Rameses tensed up in Lulu's arms; she held on to him tightly. 'French, could you just try to—'

'...EVERY TIME I TRY TO TELL YOU ONE THING,' yelled Frenchy, 'SOMETHING ELSE COMES THROUGH.'

Lulu looked around again at Owl Lady and winced. The old woman shook her head and went 'tut-tut-tut!'

'French, I don't think you realise it,' Lulu muttered under her breath, 'but you're speaking *way too loud*. The old gal over there thinks you're completely barking!'

Frenchy stood up. 'BARKING? THAT'S IN ESSEX! WE'D BETTER GET OFF, WE'VE GONE TOO FAR!'

Oh boy, what have I done? thought Lulu, feeling guilty now for getting Frenchy to do her dirty work for her. She pulled her back down into her seat. 'Sit down! All I was saying was, try to keep your voice down,' she enunciated slowly and clearly.

'WHAT? OH!' Frenchy clapped her hand to her mouth. 'I'm sorry,' she whispered.

'Look, I won't talk to you for a bit, OK?' said Lulu. 'And you don't have to tell me anything. Just give yourself time to get used to it.'

Frenchy settled down and took a deep breath. 'Yup, right...used to it.' She closed her eyes, as if to aid the process. 'How'm I going to get used to *this*?' she muttered to herself. 'The boy has a mind like a sewer!'

Lulu bit her lip. 'Uh, one other thing,' she added after a moment. 'Just tell me anything important, OK?'

'Sure thing,' said Frenchy, still with her eyes closed.

Brambly Way

Half an hour later they arrived in Hackney. Now the full effect of the Hush Brownies became evident; as they stepped off the bus their footsteps made literally *no sound at all*. Even the normal swishing sounds of clothing were, amazingly, completely silenced. It was as if Lulu and Frenchy had been transformed into two human Creeping Crillows; Lulu felt as if she were walking on air. She clicked her fingers; not the faintest sound emerged. 'It's the next best thing to being invisible!' she exclaimed.

Rameses began sniffing the air intently, craning his neck to catch as much as he could of the Hackney atmosphere; his ears twitched like radars. Lulu put him down. 'Let's watch him again, and see where he wants to go now.'

After a brief pause, Rameses started walking confidently southwards. 'Well, that's the direction of Cassandra's house,' said Lulu.

'And who knows what else,' added Frenchy. She had begun to adjust to downloading Torquil's thoughts and found that she could just about hold a conversation at the same time.

They began following Rameses.

'So what's Torquil up to now?' asked Lulu tentatively.

'Still trick-or-treating, as far as I can tell,' said Frenchy. Torquil had apparently left the house a few minutes earlier, with a 'Bye, Mum' thought-wave that strongly indicated that Varaminta was at home.

Lulu sighed. 'Doesn't sound as if he's going to be any use at all,' she said despondently.

'You never know,' said Frenchy, 'we've got several hours yet before the sweets wear off – oh, *Torquil*!'

'Now what?'

'He's just gloating at having upset some poor old lady...*shame on you*!'

'He can't hear you, French,' Lulu pointed out.

'I know, but...that is so *mean*! It seems he and his friends make a point of visiting the houses that *don't* have the jack-o'-lanterns outside, just to annoy people who want to be left alone.'

Lulu shook her head. 'That's Torquil all right.'

'Sounds as if they're also spray-painting Halloween stencils all over the vacant houses.'

'Achh!' said Lulu. 'Well, I hope they get report—'

'Oh!' cried Frenchy, suddenly stopping in her tracks.

'What?'

Frenchy stepped away and held her head in her hands again. 'Wait…wait.' She scrunched up her face in concentration.

Lulu and Rameses obediently stood and waited.

Frenchy was silent for a moment, then said, 'OK, it seems to be a phone call…'

'Yes?'

'I'm just going to relay everything back as it comes through: "Oh, this sucks…just when we were getting going…do I have to?…OK Mum, I'm coming…guys, I've gotta split…(don't tell them the truth; well not the whole truth, anyway)…I'm needed for some urgent business negotiations…top secret! (Yeah, that's cool)…"' Frenchy fell silent.

'Is that it?'

'I'm just getting repeats now…I think the phone call's finished…'

'Top secret business negotiations!' echoed Lulu. She gave a low whistle and rubbed her hands together. 'Sounds interesting!'

Frenchy still stood frowning, hand pinching her forehead. 'Yes, but I…I can't tell if that's the truth, or just what he's telling his mates.'

'OK, well, keep listening,' said Lulu. 'Uh, not that you have any choice,' she added, sheepishly.

They continued on their way, and moments later, Lulu said, 'Oh, look where we are: Field Lane. We *are* going to Cassandra's place.'

Rameses slowed down as they approached the familiar house, his ears twitching again. Cassandra's London taxi cab stood outside, but as they approached the front door with its Egyptian Pharaoh knocker, Lulu had a strong sensation that Cassandra herself was not at home. All the same, she was about to ring the doorbell, when Rameses let out an ominous growl.

Lulu and Frenchy both turned to look at him. Once again, his back was arched, and his fur stood on end, as he continued with his hostile rumblings.

Frenchy took hold of Lulu's arm. 'Don't ring,' she whispered. 'Rameses obviously senses something...or some*one*! If there's an intruder, we'll need to sneak up on them.'

Lulu felt a shiver run through her. She peered at the windows; the curtains were drawn, as always, but there appeared to be no light coming from inside. 'None of this makes sense,' she whispered. 'Cassandra was always so careful about protecting herself from intruders...unlike me.'

Rameses growled again. 'But listen to him,' insisted Frenchy. 'He's definitely picking up some nasty stuff.'

'Maybe we should go round the back,' said Lulu. 'Down that footpath.'

Frenchy looked at the cat. 'I'm worried he could give us away, though. It's all very well being silenced by the Hush Brownies, but if he growls or hisses...'

Lulu bit her lip. 'But he's the one who can lead us to Cassandra...besides, there's no way we could shake him off even if we tried. Oh wow, how did I manage to get us into this mess?'

'OK, let's go round the back,' said Frenchy at last. 'Is your phone switched off?'

Lulu's hands were shaking as she took out her phone and turned it off. 'OK. I'm ready.'

The cold night air was almost eerily still, an effect heightened by their silent steps, and the gathering mist under the moonless sky. Focus on your star, Lulu told herself, as they crept back down the road a little way, towards the entrance to the footpath.

Your star, which speaks to you across time and space...

The words from *The Apple Star* echoed around her brain. The effect was reassuring, yet a painful reminder of her loss.

The narrow footpath, lit only by the occasional dingy yellow lamp, was overhung with brambles and had a ripe, earthy smell. They followed it down between two houses, then around the corner into the part that led along the backs of the gardens.

They were about three gardens away from Cassandra's, when Lulu saw something that made her heart leap. A large, shadowy figure was emerging from Cassandra's garden gate. And it definitely wasn't Cassandra.

Grassy Hideout

Lulu just managed to suppress a squeal. She grabbed Frenchy by the arm, and together with Rameses they raced silently back down the path and around the corner. There was not the slightest sound to draw attention to their presence – Lulu prayed they hadn't been spotted. The girls backed into the prickly brambles, concealing themselves as best they could as the heavy footsteps approached. Rameses, on the other hand, stood frozen in the middle of the path, staring defiantly at the oncoming stranger. He hissed loudly.

'Gertcha!' growled the stranger as he stomped heavily forth; Rameses leapt out of the way. The man, Lulu saw as he emerged, was not alone; there were two of them – big blond men – and they were carrying a large crate. For a terrifying moment, Lulu felt sure she and Frenchy would be seen as the men turned the corner. But they did not turn; instead, they continued in the same direction, pausing to open a chain-link gate. They looked like the men who had followed them from school in the van – and now Lulu saw something which left her in no doubt at all: a golden fish-tailed horse with crown emblazoned on the nearest man's sleeve. The contents of the crate rattled around, and Lulu could see the tops of the large jars Cassandra stored her dry ingredients in; they were stealing her stuff! But where was Cassandra herself…?

Now the men passed through the gate into a different section of the path, one that Lulu had not known existed. She counted in her head; *ten, nine, eight* – the heavy footsteps retreated – *three, two, one.* 'Phew!' she breathed out heavily.

'Sh, hang on!' whispered Frenchy. 'There might be more of them.' She peered around the corner. 'Nope…OK, let's go.'

Lulu felt almost paralysed with anxiety about Cassandra now, but somehow she managed to follow Frenchy through the chain-link gate after the men. Thank heaven for Hush Brownies, she thought. Soft-pawed as he was, Rameses was more soundless than even the most nimble of cats, due to having had a taste of the Hush Brownies himself. Lulu was desperate to ask Frenchy if she had got any more information on Torquil, but talking was definitely not an option.

The path was dark and overgrown, but soon Lulu caught sight of moving shadows up ahead. The three of them continued to follow, and after a few moments Lulu could see that the path was coming to an end. The men disappeared momentarily into open space; this would be the risky part. The girls paused at the end of the path, where some stone steps led down to a sloping bank of grassland. Beyond that, mist swirling up from it, was water: a canal. The men were carrying the crate towards a large narrow boat.

At this point, Lulu judged that the men were far enough in the distance not to hear her voice. 'Now what?' she whispered.

'We stow away on that boat.'

Lulu's heart did a flip. 'Are you crazy?'

'Lu, we've got to find out what's going on. This is the only way.'

Lulu watched as the men hoisted the crate onto the boat. She thought her legs would give way with nerves. 'What about Torquil?' she asked, hopefully. 'Have you got anything more on this secret business thingy?'

Frenchy shook her head. 'I'm not getting much; the signals seem to be fading. I think I might be losing contact.'

'Oh great,' said Lulu flatly. 'Then he can't have taken all three sweets.'

'Lu!' said Frenchy suddenly. 'The men, look! They're coming back! We've got to hide.'

'Where?' asked Lulu, looking desperately around; there was not a tree or building in sight. 'Back down the path!' she suggested, but Frenchy shook her head.

'No...look, see that pile of junk over there?' she said, nodding in the direction of some rubbish: a supermarket trolley and a sprawl of unidentifiable masses on the grass.

Lulu felt ill. 'You're out of your mind!' she protested. 'There's probably rats in there!'

But the men were drawing closer now. 'Lu, we don't have any choice,' insisted Frenchy. 'We can spread ourselves out, just pretend to *be* rubbish.' She crouched down, pulling Lulu with her, and the two of them edged silently away from the path. At least they couldn't be heard – and Lulu was thankful for the long grass, the mist, and the fact that the moon still hadn't risen. Then they lay down, limbs tucked in, hoping they looked more like piles of old clothes than dead bodies.

As she lay there, face down in the grass beside some mouldy curtains, Lulu wondered what Dad would think of all this. He would be horrified, of course; what was more, he would be expecting her home in about an hour's time. At this rate, there was no way that was going to happen.

The shuffling noises of the passing men approached, then retreated. Lulu waited motionless until they were well away, then lifted her head. 'French?'

'I'm here,' said Frenchy. 'You OK?'

'Er, yeah, I guess.'

'Right,' whispered Frenchy. 'Time to get on that boat. My guess is, they've gone back to Cassandra's for another crate, so this is our perfect chance.'

Lulu pulled her phone from her pocket and switched it on. 'Just a minute.' She sent Dad a text message:

PARTY GOES ON LATER THAN I THOUGHT...BACK BY 10, OK? L X

'Come on, Lu! We've got no time to lose!'

Lulu switched off her phone and put it away. 'OK, I'm coming!'

Rameses, who had been patiently sitting nearby, stood up and joined them as they headed down to the boat. But as they drew nearer, they noticed a dim light shining inside the boat; there seemed to be someone else on board.

Lulu and Frenchy threw themselves back down onto the grass. 'OK, now what?' hissed Lulu.

'I was wondering the same thing,' whispered Frenchy. 'Also, it's all very well having our movements silenced by the Hush Brownies, but how do we avoid *rocking the boat*?'

'Oh blimey, you're right,' groaned Lulu.

'There's only one thing for it,' said Frenchy at last. 'We have to board at exactly the same time as the men do.'

Lulu stared at her in disbelief. 'French, how on *earth* are we going to do that?'

'We jump off that bridge,' said Frenchy, nodding in the direction of a low footbridge. 'Look, the back end of the boat is really near it. They're loading up at the front end.' The boat was long – maybe twenty metres – and there was a small deck area at each end. In between was the cabin, high enough to block any view the men might have of the girls…as long as they timed their jump *very* carefully.

Watery Surprise

Looking out through the bridge's railings down onto the boat, two things occurred to Lulu, one good…and one not so good. The good thing was that the bridge was even lower than she had thought; they might not have to jump after all. The not-so-good thing was, she had no idea how they would climb over the railings without being seen. The combination of Hush Brownies, darkness and mist had enabled them to get this far apparently without being noticed by whoever was on the boat. But there would be no such camouflage when they were right out in the open, not twenty metres away from the enemy.

Lulu glanced anxiously at Frenchy, desperate to speak; by the look on Frenchy's face, she felt the same way too. Meanwhile, the two men had reappeared and were approaching with another crate; Lulu felt Rameses rumble in her arms as he let out another low growl. *Oh, please be quiet!* thought Lulu.

She watched, feeling increasingly helpless, as the men began loading the crate onto the boat; she and Frenchy were still without a workable plan. The first man boarded, then the second one. Then they disappeared from sight, behind the cabin. Lulu and Frenchy looked at each other, then began to get up, but ducked down again when one man reappeared, approached the tether rope and began to cast off. The engine started up. The girls waited for him to finish casting off; they were going to have to move *very* quickly.

Suddenly Rameses wriggled wildly in Lulu's arms; before she knew what was happening, he leapt onto the boat from between the railings, at exactly the moment the man withdrew.

It was now or never; Lulu and Frenchy scrambled over the railings. Frenchy slipped down onto the boat; her feet touched the deck before she even had to let go. Lulu followed. She was almost in contact with the deck when, horrified, she felt a jerk; her skirt was caught on a broken railing. The boat began to move away. Lulu tugged and tugged, eventually ripping the delicate muslin to free herself, but now her feet were dangling over the canal.

Then something wonderful happened; the boat reversed ever so slightly; just enough to allow her to plop down softly and collapse in a heap. They were on their way.

*

The cry of a moorhen pierced the darkness as the boat chugged steadily through black water. Ghostly grey shapes of swans hovered in the mist. They passed a disused warehouse, swanky apartment blocks and non-swanky lorry depots. The moist night air penetrated the thin fabric of Lulu's dress, and she wished she had a coat. Lulu could hear the muffled voices of the men inside the cabin. Occasionally she could make out what was being said, but it was nothing interesting; they seemed to be puzzling over a crossword. She took the pen and pad from Frenchy's backpack and wrote:

Anything more from Torquil?

She showed it to Frenchy.

Frenchy just shook her head.

Lulu put the pad back in the backpack. She watched Rameses; so poised and regal, he had the air of being supremely confident and in control. She wished she felt the same.

Then the sound of rushing water gave Lulu another mild jolt of panic; they were approaching a lock. She realised she should have thought of this possibility before; she and Dad had been on canal pleasure cruises before now, and going up or down in this waterway equivalent of a lift was always the most enjoyable part. This time it posed a risk; one of the men might see them when he got out to operate the lock. When the boat stopped, Lulu and Frenchy crouched down as low as possible and waited.

The whole process seemed to take forever, but when they got moving again – thankfully undetected – Lulu was surprised to find that no more than ten minutes had passed.

Gradually the depots and factories gave way to more and more swanky apartment blocks, and Lulu could make out the blinking red light on the familiar triangular roof of Canary Wharf's Canada Tower; they were approaching the river Thames. The banks on either side of the canal began to narrow, and glistening black stone walls were closing in on them. Rushing water heralded the approach of another lock.

Then the boat did something unexpected; instead of heading straight for the lock, it began to veer to the left. Lulu and Frenchy exchanged glances; even Rameses stood up and began pacing around, agitated. Lulu shut her eyes tight; concentrate on your star, she told herself. Let it be your guide.

The boat went on turning.

Let your star be your guide.

Lulu opened her eyes; the boat had turned a full ninety degrees, and was now directly facing the looming black wall, where she now saw there was a large iron gate. Above it was something that looked a lot like a security camera. As the gate began to grind open, it became clear that if they didn't want to be seen, they had no choice; they had to get off the boat, and fast. They were lucky; now that the boat had turned, they were not more than a metre from the lock, and solid ground.

Lulu and Frenchy looked at each other, then jumped; Rameses followed. They crept along the top of the wall to the base of some stone steps, where they crouched and watched as the gate continued to crank open. It gave onto a tunnel, inside which were two more men with torches. They shone them directly onto the boat, inspecting every part of it; Lulu saw the security camera move as it followed the boat's progress. As the boat entered the tunnel, and the gate began to close behind it, Lulu didn't know whether to rejoice that they had got off in time, or shake her fists in frustration.

'Boy, that was a close one!' gasped Frenchy, as soon as it was safe to talk.

'Right,' said Lulu, with some irony. 'But where the heck do we go from here?'

Meat Hook Lane

'Lu, get out the pen and pad, will you?' said Frenchy, handing Lulu her backpack as she scrunched her face up with concentration.

Lulu hurriedly fished around in the bag. 'Are you getting more signals?' she asked eagerly.

'Yes! Have been for about the last twenty minutes, but I couldn't say anything,' said Frenchy. 'Seems as if Torquil ate the other two sweets.'

'Blimey, it's not like him to take that long,' remarked Lulu.

Frenchy frowned, deep in concentration. 'Something happened to make him want those other wishes, I think; ones he was saving for later. Hang on...crikey, this is hard!'

Lulu sat, pen poised. She watched Rameses as he sniffed around; he was either taking stock of the situation before deciding on a direction...or else he hadn't a clue where to go next. 'Take your time,'

Lulu told Frenchy, forcing herself to be patient.

Frenchy put her fingers to her temples. 'OK...right now he's in a discussion with some people ...Varaminta's there...'

Lulu jotted this down. 'Are they at home?'

'No...they went somewhere. By taxi, I think. There's a man...Roman; his name seems to be Roman...Fisher. I think that's it; he seems to be dominating the discussion.'

Lulu wrote down the name. 'What's it about?'

'Money, mostly...there's a lot of stuff about percentages and so on...Torquil seems to be very involved in the bargaining process...'

'Why am I not surprised?' remarked Lulu.

'Hold on...' Frenchy knitted her brow as she concentrated on the information as it came through. 'This is...this is definitely connected to *The Apple Star*...'

Lulu felt her ears tingle with excitement. 'Are you sure?'

'I'm getting *The Apple Star*, yes...Torquil and Varaminta seem to have it with them. This is becoming very heated...oh, it's making my head hurt!'

'Do you have any clues as to *where* they are, French?' Lulu asked softly, trying not to add to Frenchy's headache.

'Where?' said Frenchy, vaguely. 'Oh, it's like a thunderstorm in my head!' she cried. 'Torquil's …making demands.'

'Just try and get something about *where*, French…'

'It hurts, it hurts!' cried Frenchy, clutching her head in her hands. 'Oh!' She doubled up.

Lulu stroked her back, not knowing what else to do. The effect the Psychic Psours and Medium Sweets were having on Frenchy was really beginning to worry her, and she felt guiltier than ever for using her. Think about your star, she told herself, hoping once again that this might help. Gazing into Rameses' eyes as she thought, she was reminded of the message from Cassandra. She looked in the backpack, and found the note. She read it over again:

IF THIS HAS REACHED YOU, IT MEANS I AM IN DANGER — PROBABLY FROM MY COUSIN, OMAR RISHNEF. FIND HIM AND YOU WILL FIND ME. CASSANDRA.

'Find him and you will find me…' she whispered. She found herself staring at that name, somehow fixated on it. Omar Rishnef…

She laid the slip of paper on the notepad. There was something about that name... She lined it up above the one she had just written down:

OMAR RISHNEF
Roman Fisher

'Of course!' she cried. 'It's an anagram!'

Frenchy looked up. 'What is?'

'Roman Fisher, Omar Rishnef...it's the same person, don't you see? He must have changed his name, but all he did was move the letters around.' She began ticking off each letter in 'Roman Fisher'; sure enough, it fitted. 'It *has* to be him, it's too much of a coincidence! French, you realise what this means, don't you?'

Frenchy, her face still pale and agonised from the turmoil of the Torquil thought-waves, managed a nod. 'Yes...somehow I *have* to find out from Torquil where he is.'

Lulu squeezed her arm. 'Yes, oh *please*! All this time, we thought we were following two different trails...and it turns out it's the same one! Cassandra, Varaminta and Torquil with *The Apple Star*, Roman/Omar...and those men on the narrow boat...they're all in the same place!'

Frenchy winced. 'Oh, it hurts so much!'

Lulu thought some more. 'We're near...very near,' she mused, staring at the pavement. Somewhere underground...

'Then Rameses...ought to be able to help,' said Frenchy.

'Maybe if we start walking,' suggested Lulu, 'he might start picking up a scent somewhere.'

'OK,' agreed Frenchy, getting up. 'You know what else? From now on, I'm screening Torquil out.'

Lulu looked uncertain. 'Can you do that?'

'I'm going to try,' said Frenchy, taking off her glasses and rubbing her eyes. 'All this money talk is just going around in circles; it's not helping us at all. What I need to do is try...try to recall more of his thoughts from when he was on his *way* to where he is now; they haven't been there long.'

'Well if you can, French, you might be able to ease the headache.'

Frenchy put her glasses back on and nodded, sighing. 'Yup; here's hoping. Come on.'

They went up a cobbled street that led them under a railway viaduct; Lulu looked up and saw a grimy old sign. '"Meat Hook Lane"; French, does that ring any bells?'

'I'm thinking,' said Frenchy. 'There was a whole jumble of information...he seemed to have been thinking about some awful horror movie at one point...I think there *was* a meat hook...'

A train rumbled overhead as they emerged beside a boarded-up building site. 'Building site!' said Frenchy suddenly. 'That's right – it's coming back to me now. There was definitely something in Torquil's thoughts about a boarded-up site. This was the first thing they had to look for after they got out of the taxi...yes, and I got "underneath the arches" – which this is. OK, and the next thing they had to find was...railings!' As if to confirm this, Rameses found a gap in the boards where some iron railings were exposed, and disappeared between them.

'Rameses!' called Lulu in a loud whisper. But Rameses wouldn't come; instead he just miaowed. Frenchy squeezed through the tiny gap and went after him; Lulu followed, struggling a little with her skirts. She had just wiggled herself free when Frenchy cried, 'Lu! Check this out!'

Open Sesame

Lulu peered at the thing Frenchy was so excited about: a circular piece of ironwork set into the pavement. 'OK, it's a manhole cover. And…?'

'This is the entrance, Lu!' cried Frenchy. 'This is how we get in!'

Lulu scratched her head. 'How do you know?'

'Look at it, Lu. What does it say?'

'TOWER HAMLETS…LONDON,' read Lulu.

'Yes, yes, but what about the bit in the middle?'

Lulu peered closer. 'Oh! ELF KING? Hang on, that can't be right…oh, it's "SELF-LOCKING". The "S" and the "LOC" are practically worn away.'

'Right,' said Frenchy. 'Well, this was the next thing, I'm sure of it!' Frenchy was almost cross-eyed with concentration. 'Look, I know it was a while back, and I didn't get to jot anything down, but – yes, I'm absolutely positive I got "Look for the sign of the Elf King". At the time I thought I must have understood it wrong; I mean, "elf king" – *really*. But now it makes sense!'

In spite of her anxiety – or perhaps because of it – Lulu couldn't help giggling as the ludicrous image of an elf king impressed itself on her mind. 'Why do I feel as if I've strayed into a Tolkien story?'

Frenchy, however, looked deadly serious as she ran her fingers over the letters. 'This is it, all right…they've gone down here.'

Lulu gazed at her in disbelief. 'You are kidding. Get Varaminta down a manhole? In designer cashmere and stilettos? No way!'

'I'm telling you, that's what I got!' insisted Frenchy. 'Just look at Rameses. He knows.'

Rameses looked up from his intense sniffing of the spot, and miaowed in response.

Lulu stared blankly at the heavy old lump of metal. 'I haven't the slightest idea how to open a manhole cover.'

Frenchy paused. 'No – wait; if I remember correctly…I think there's some kind of switch.' She reached inside one of the holes in the manhole cover.

'You need one of those thingies they use,' said Lulu, miming the use of a lifting key.

Frenchy said nothing, just kept feeling inside the holes. 'Ah! Here it is…'

There was a soft *click*, and Lulu watched in amazement as the words 'ELF KING' slowly began to rotate, accompanied by a low humming sound. As it turned, the manhole cover raised itself up, attached to two metal supports. It went on rising until it came up to Lulu's hips, then stopped.

'There's your entrance!' Frenchy announced proudly.

Lulu shook her head slowly. 'Amazing.' Rameses stood at the edge of the deep shaft that appeared before them and sniffed inside.

Frenchy took hold of him and climbed down onto the rungs of an iron ladder attached to the wall of the shaft. 'Well, come on!' she urged.

Lulu stared into the chasm, unable to move. 'Just a minute,' she called back.

'What's up?'

'I'm just...a bit claustrophobic, that's all,' Lulu replied. Her breathing quickened. She shut her eyes and clenched her fists. She was afraid, it was true, but less of the confined space than of what they would face down below. Because right now she was getting a very familiar twisting sensation in her belly... And what if Roman Fisher knew someone had entered, and immediately set his guards onto them? But they had got this far, and the longer she hesitated, the greater the danger...

'Lu, come on!' came Frenchy's anxious voice.

Consumed with anxiety though she was, Lulu realised she had no choice; she picked up Rameses and stepped inside.

*

They descended in silence through the gloomy, damp-smelling shaft, afraid to make a sound. Lulu felt a sudden surge of panic as she realised that now, even if she wanted to make that emergency call to Dad, she wouldn't be able to; down here there would be no signal. 'Oh my God...' she whispered, in spite of herself. Cut off completely. Or was she? All of a sudden she remembered with excitement that she still had some spare Medium Sweets in her pocket. That's it! she thought: she could eat them, then transmit her thoughts to Dad...but then her heart sank as she realised she had no way of explaining to him about the Psychic Psours up in the wardrobe, and getting him to take them. Without those, the Medium Sweets by themselves would be useless.

Lulu took a deep breath; think positive, she told herself. Nothing will go wrong, and you won't have to contact Dad.

Now they had reached the bottom of the shaft, and

began heading down the solitary tunnel, their steps still silenced by the Hush Brownies. Rameses quickly took the lead, striding forth confidently, ears twitching. Once again, Lulu found herself wishing she could be just as bold and fearless. But she was somewhat reassured by the thought that they must have got in undetected, since no one had come after them yet. She supposed that if this really was the entrance, it was unguarded because no one could ever possibly find it unless they were in the know. Either that, or Frenchy had got things muddled up, and this bizarre trail was in fact leading them nowhere...

They rounded a bend, and now the tunnel divided into two. Rameses paused; the girls waited. The cat circled around, tail flicking as if it were picking up radio waves, then headed down the right-hand passageway. This sloped down quite steeply, and the girls had to run to keep him in sight; even when running, their footsteps made not the slightest wisp of a sound. But then, as the tunnel began to level out, Lulu saw something that made her turn hot and cold at the same time. They were close to the end of the tunnel, which seemed to open out into a bigger space, and just appearing was the lower half of a pair of black-trousered legs. They seemed to belong to a man seated on a chair. Frenchy had seen them too, and immediately the girls began to retreat back up the tunnel. When they had gone far enough to be out of sight, and it was clear they weren't being followed, they stopped and looked around; they couldn't see Rameses.

Seconds later, they heard a gruff man's voice, apparently addressing the cat. 'How did you get down 'ere then, eh?' Rameses miaowed in response.

Then came a voice that Lulu knew only too well: Cassandra's. Incredibly, her voice was just as deep and calm as ever, greeting Rameses as if she had never seen him. 'Oh, what a lovely cat,' she said.

Green Sweet Panic

'All right mog, outcha get!' barked the man.

Lulu, listening from up the sloping passage, thought he must have picked Rameses up – very roughly, no doubt, for the next thing she heard was the combined screeches and yowls of both cat and man, echoing up the tunnel. 'OWWW! Come 'ere, you little *rat*!' This was followed by loud thumping, as the man apparently chased Rameses who had, it seemed, shot off in a different direction. The footsteps grew fainter and fainter. Not caring any more that the man might return at any moment, Lulu rushed silently down the tunnel to where she found Cassandra imprisoned in a steel-gated cell; Frenchy followed.

Cassandra reached through the bars for Lulu's hand and squeezed it. 'Bless you,' she said softly. She didn't seem surprised at all; Lulu realised that the moment she saw Rameses, she would have understood that he had brought help – and then cleverly diverted the guard. Cassandra glanced around furtively. 'We haven't much time; he'll be back any moment. I notice you're making no sound; have you both had Hush Brownies?'

Lulu and Frenchy nodded.

Cassandra was impressed. 'Excellent! I told you they were good for emergencies, didn't I? Right, here's what I want you to do: one of you has to sneak up behind him and get the swipe card that unlocks this gate…he keeps it in the back pocket of his trousers. Don't worry about him turning around or sitting down; I'll handle that. Just get the card; now hide in that locker – quick!'

Lulu looked and saw that Cassandra was indicating a tall locker beside the guard's chair. It was a squeeze, but she and Frenchy were just able to fit inside, keeping the door slightly ajar, from which Lulu could view the man's movements.

'What happened to the cat?' Cassandra casually asked the man when he returned.

'Lost 'im,' he sniffed, about to sit down again.

'Could I have a quiet word?' said Cassandra, beckoning him over.

The man paused. 'What is it?'

'Sh!' hissed Cassandra. The man moved closer, and Cassandra began to whisper to him. Lulu couldn't take it all in, but there was something about being willing to talk…and she seemed to be interesting him in some sort of deal that would make him personally rich; it was this part that kept him keenly interested long enough for Lulu to step forward silently, remove the card from his pocket, and slip back into the locker.

When Cassandra saw that Lulu was safely back inside, she made a start, as if in reaction to a sudden noise in the tunnel Lulu and Frenchy had come from. 'What's that?' she hissed.

'What?' said the man.

'I think I heard some movement up there…it could be an intruder; perhaps they used that cat as a decoy.'

This prompted immediate action from the man; he bolted swiftly up the tunnel. As soon as he was far enough away, Lulu sprang forward and swiped the card where Cassandra showed her to put it; the gate swung open. Cassandra gently closed the gate, and quickly guided Lulu and Frenchy down the other tunnel. This had several empty enclosures leading off it; Cassandra dived into one of them and led the girls behind a stack of crates. She leaned against them and sighed deeply, her hand to her chest. She looked exhausted, Lulu thought, but otherwise much the same; still dressed in her flowing robes, she maintained a quiet dignity about her.

'Oh girls, girls…' Cassandra said at last. 'I never thought Rameses would seek *you* out!'

Lulu frowned. 'You didn't?'

Cassandra looked mortified. 'Oh, good heavens, no! I feel terrible about it. Terrible! There are any number of adults he could have gone to.'

'But we *wanted* to help,' said Frenchy.

'Besides, we've got to get *The Apple Star* back,' added Lulu.

Cassandra looked taken aback. '*The Apple Star*? Oh, I was afraid of that! I had a feeling... they've stolen it, haven't they? Varaminta and Torquil?'

'You knew?' asked Lulu.

'Not exactly,' said Cassandra. 'But now that you mention it...and they're here, now?'

'Yes.'

Cassandra shook her head. 'Oh, I wish I could have warned you!'

Lulu had wondered about this. 'But with your second sight, and everything...?'

'It has its limitations,' explained Cassandra. 'Concentrate your energies in one area – Omar in this case – and you'll miss what's going on elsewhere. What I can do is get *The Apple Star* back for you...but right now, you must leave.'

'Oh no, we can't leave you now!' Lulu insisted. 'Or Rameses...wherever he is.'

'Rameses will be fine,' said Cassandra, 'and so will I. Now listen; you know the tunnel you took from the street to my cell; it divides into two, am I right?'

'Yes.'

'All right,' said Cassandra. 'The guard will first have checked the entrance, then taken the other tunnel, the most direct route to the main chamber, and checked around there. Then he'll come back up this way, checking each enclosure. The whole thing takes about fifteen minutes; I've timed it. That gives you about ten minutes to go back out the way you came; go, it'll be clear now.'

Lulu and Frenchy looked at each other. 'I'm sorry,' said Lulu. 'I can't do it…I just can't!'

'You *have* to,' said Cassandra, quite stern now. 'I know exactly how to get *The Apple Star* back, I promise. You've helped me, now I'll help you…get home safely, please!'

Frenchy pulled on Lulu's arm. 'Lu, she's right …come on.'

Lulu thought about all she had put Frenchy through. Was it really fair to endanger her further? And they *had* helped Cassandra a bit, at least. Glancing at her watch, she saw it was almost ten; Dad would start to worry soon; he would try to phone and be unable to reach her. Then he would call Frenchy's mum, and the friend who was not really having a party...then the police...

Lulu felt tears come to her eyes as she gave Cassandra a hug. Unable to say a word, she allowed herself to be led away by Frenchy. Then the two of them ran as fast as they could, back to the entrance. Even as she ran, Lulu still felt herself torn in two; leaving Cassandra and *The Apple Star* – and Rameses, for that matter – felt wrong, wrong, wrong.

Cassandra was right; they got to the bottom of the entrance shaft without being seen. But as they began to climb, Lulu heard footsteps approaching.

'Hurry!' squeaked Frenchy from behind her. 'Someone's coming!'

'I know!' hissed Lulu, her heart thumping as she climbed as fast as she could. Again she cursed her voluminous Halloween skirts as they bunched around her legs. She peered up in the dank gloom, but the manhole wasn't in sight yet.

Then the ladder jolted; someone heavy had got on at the bottom. Lulu scrambled up for all she was worth, straining her eyes for the manhole. A few more steps and then, at last, it appeared. Now, if she could just make out where the switch was...

The heavy footfalls rang out on the iron rungs below; *thunk, thunk, thunk...*

Another thought surfaced in Lulu's mind: *phone Dad.* But *how*? The complicated manoeuvres necessary to pull out her phone, switch it on and make a call the instant they reached the surface – while still trying to escape – how on earth would she do it?

Ker-thunk, *ker*-thunk…now there seemed to be two of them.

Lulu fumbled around the manhole for the switch, and found it; she flicked it, but then she had to wait wait wait for the manhole to unscrew itself and open up. A heavy lump formed in Lulu's belly as the awful realisation dawned on her: *we don't stand a chance of getting away now…*

Forced to wait, she could at least make that phone call now; she took out her phone and switched it on. The little screen lit up; she waited for the signal, which seemed to take forever. She held the phone higher, while at the same time feeling around in her pocket for those spare Medium Sweets.

The manhole cover rose higher, and *bing!* There was the signal…Lulu squeezed through the gap. She was half out, phone in one hand and Medium Sweet in the other, when Frenchy screamed.

Lulu speed-dialled Dad, who answered instantly, 'Lulu!'

'Dad, you've got to eat the green sweets!' blurted

Lulu, ignoring Dad's urgent inquiries about where she was. 'The green sweets!' she shouted again – then gasped as a hand grabbed her leg – 'The wardrobe...attic...key's on my de—' The hand on her leg yanked her down and she cried out, dropping the phone.

The sweet...she still had the sweet. Shutting her eyes and praying, Lulu ate it.

Roman Fisher

'Poodle! How the heck did you get here?' Torquil's blood-red mouth leered darkly, his teeth yellow against his whitened Dracula face. He looked both surprised and amused.

Lulu said nothing; she was still busy transmitting thought-waves to Dad, instructing him on how to find her and Frenchy. She had been doing so from the moment they were captured, but needed to repeat the thoughts over and over, to make sure they reached him. *Tower Hamlets…Meat Hook Lane…building site…manhole…*

'We flew,' said Frenchy, sarcastically. 'First class.'

The two guards who had caught them wore black overalls; adorning the sleeves was, of course, the familiar logo of golden fish-tailed horse and crown. They had escorted the girls to the office of Roman Fisher Enterprises, a vaulted chamber that overlooked a small quadrangle adjacent to the underground canal. Moored in the canal basin was the narrow boat Lulu and Frenchy had stowed away on, and a little way off was the big gate it had come through. And as well as Dracula-Torquil, Varaminta and one other guard there was, of course, Roman Fisher.

He didn't fit the picture Lulu had formed in her mind at all; in fact she found it quite impossible to believe this man had once been a humble Moroccan fisherman. The only thing remotely humble about Roman Fisher was his stature: he was very short. How appropriate for an elf king, Lulu couldn't help thinking. And he was certainly dressed well enough for royalty; in contrast to the rather rickety old desk he was leaning on, the man himself would have impressed even the *Fashion Police*. His outfit said 'English Gentleman' – or rather, yelled it through a loud-hailer. His slicked-back hair was as glossy as his leather shoes, and his candy-striped shirt had such a high, stiff collar, Lulu wondered if he was actually able to turn his head. She couldn't remember the last time she'd seen a man in a three-piece pinstripe suit, complete with buttonhole and watch chain. Alongside the huge gormless boiler-suited guards, he looked like their shiny new toy.

'Ugh, I don't believe this!' snorted Varaminta. She was seated on a very un-Varaminta-like ripped plastic office chair, but otherwise looked as pristine as ever in a pea-green jersey dress and black patent boots. In one arm she held Poochie, her ridiculous little dog, in its very own little designer Halloween outfit: a black jumper encrusted with diamante moons and stars, with a matching bow on its head. With her other hand, Varaminta clutched to her chest the modest little yellow-bound book: *The Apple Star*. 'Look, they've obviously followed us here, but I suggest we just send them on their way and get on with business.'

'Wait, wait...' said Roman Fisher. 'Indulge me a while, dear lady, I have some questions.' His voice was as polished as marble.

'Forget it!' Lulu interrupted angrily. 'Give up your nasty scheme now; my dad's on his way, and he's got the police with him.'

Varaminta let out a peal of derisive laughter. 'Ha! But of course he is! The girl's a fantasist, Roman; a truly over-active imagination.'

'*Grrr – yap!*' added Halloween Poochie, for effect.

'It's *true*,' Frenchy protested. 'And that book belongs to Lulu; you stole it! I'm sure the police would be very interested to know how you came by it.'

Roman raised his eyebrows at Varaminta. 'Well, well!' he uttered admiringly. 'You fascinate me more every minute, Miss le B. But I'm sorry, we can't really just let these little waifs go, now they're here. Much too...hmm, volatile.'

'Give me my book back!' yelled Lulu. The guard tightened his grip.

'Oh, shut up!' snapped Roman Fisher, his smarm suddenly giving way to anger. 'Your type make me sick! You're so *worthy*; I suppose you think you've inherited some sort of "special gift", do you? Think you're carrying on a tradition of *do-gooders*, just like that, that—'

'Cassandra?' said Lulu.

'Oh, you know her, eh?'

'Your cousin,' said Frenchy.

Roman Fisher looked momentarily startled, then concealed his surprise. 'That's a lie,' he snapped. 'Goodness knows what other idiocies that madwoman has filled your fluffy little brains with. Ha! You're *selfish*, the lot of you – that's what you are! Thinking you're somehow uniquely entitled...well, what about the rest of us, eh? But no; as soon as someone with a halfway decent *business mind* comes along' – he jabbed at his temple – 'it's "ooh, got to protect our little secrets from the nasty bogeyman"!'

'*She's* the nasty one,' said Varaminta. 'This little minx has stirred up enough trouble for me already. Well, you're not going to succeed this time, madam! This is going to be a truly great partnership,' she went on, eyes glinting as she reached out to Roman Fisher. 'An empire, even!'

195

'A *Roman* Empire, ha ha!' added Roman Fisher, taking her hand. He looked ridiculous next to Varaminta, who towered over him. 'You see, my little do-gooders,' he went on, 'your puny dabblings cannot possibly compete with the work of a great alchemist such as myself. I have waited *years* for this moment! Until now I've had to content myself with just one ingredient...*you'd* call them Quicksilver berries.'

Lulu, her head still full of the instructions she was sending Dad, felt her ears prick up at the mention of this mind-sharpening ingredient for the Chocolate Wishes. 'Where did you get them from?'

'Ah! A secret island,' smirked Roman Fisher. 'Where money grows on trees! Here.' He threw Lulu a small packet, a little larger than a matchbox.

Lulu read the label. 'The...Midas Touch?'

'Go on.'

Lulu turned the packet over. It said:

Think that making a fortune is the preserve of the few? Well, you're wrong! A course of these 'Midas Touch' tablets, made to a unique secret recipe, will improve your moneymaking skills immeasurably!

Lulu was filled with disgust at this grotesque distortion of the true nature and purpose of the Quicksilver berries. 'I suppose you know King Midas's golden touch made him absolutely miserable?'

Roman Fisher laughed, casting a conspiratorial glance at Varaminta and Torquil. 'I knew she wouldn't appreciate my genius for marketing!' He paced towards Lulu, shaking his head in wonder. 'Stupid...stupid...' He lifted her head by the chin, his voice dripping with contempt. 'Most people are STUPID. They'll believe what they want to believe.' He took the packet back from Lulu and shook it. 'That's why something like this is so brilliant!' He strode back towards Varaminta. 'Imagine...if this is what can be done with just one ingredient, what would be possible with a whole recipe...a whole *book* full of recipes! Oh!' Roman Fisher closed his eyes, as if in ecstasy.

Lulu, to her horror, could imagine only too well.

'Yes, the master alchemist has all the elements in place now; the earth and water, or food and drink, that you see here' – he indicated the crates of ingredients plundered from Cassandra's – 'combined with this famous celestial body, *The Apple Star*, and ignited by the fiery touch of the sun, the master alchemist himself' – here he puffed out his little chest proudly – 'the result will be *pure gold*. An unlimited supply!'

Lulu could hardly believe her ears. Not only was this underworld elf king a con man, he appeared to be dangerously deluded as well. But Varaminta and Torquil were lapping it up, confident that they, too, would soon be tapping into this seam of endless wealth. She remembered how Varaminta used to boast about Torquil's moneymaking schemes; 'he'll be a millionaire before he's twenty!' she would say. It looked as if that prediction was about to come true.

'So what to do with these two, eh?' Roman Fisher went on. 'Tut tut tut...I don't know...'

'I tried bargaining with *her* before,' said Dracula-Torquil, pointing to Lulu. 'Useless!'

'She's an evil schemer,' added Varaminta.

'Hmm...' said Roman Fisher, folding his arms and scratching his chin. 'Very inconvenient...an *accident*, I think.'

The guard beside him, a great blond slab of a man, flexed his huge sausage hands in anticipation. Aware that another black-overalled figure had just entered the room, Lulu felt her skin prickle with fear.

Sausage Hands

Roman Fisher paused as he mused on exactly what kind of accident he might use to dispose of Lulu and Frenchy. The dank airlessness of the underground cavern made Lulu feel nauseous.

Suddenly, a voice from somewhere shouted 'RAT!' and a small brown furry thing darted straight for Varaminta's legs.

'Aargh!' cried Varaminta, toppling over and losing grip of both Poochie – who went into paroxysms of yapping – and *The Apple Star*. Torquil dived for it, but before Lulu knew what was happening, the guard who had just entered the room lunged forward and got it first. Meanwhile, Varaminta was still screeching as Sausage Hands tried to free her of the rat – which Lulu now saw was no rat: it was Rameses. And the 'guard' who now held *The Apple Star* was none other than Cassandra dressed in black overalls.

Torquil and Roman descended upon Cassandra.

'Stop!' she cried, holding *The Apple Star* aloft. 'Don't forget, Omar, those ingredients you've plundered from my house won't last forever; you need suppliers' information. Well, I've decided to tell you who they are.'

'I'm very glad to hear it,' said Roman Fisher, trying to ignore Poochie's continued yapping. 'But I'll thank you to call me by my name, *Roman*. What have you done with my guard?'

Cassandra shrugged. 'He'll be all right. As for you, you'll only get the information you want if this book is returned to its rightful owner, and she and her friend are set free.'

'Oh, I think that's out of the question,' chortled Roman.

'Then go ahead and take the book; you'll have dozens of recipes,' said Cassandra, dangling *The Apple Star* in front of Roman's nose. He reached for it, and she flipped it away. 'But you'll never – and I mean *never* – get a word out of me about suppliers. Not exactly enough to build that empire on, is it?'

Roman Fisher narrowed his eyes, folded his arms and paced some more. His sausage-handed guard, back at his master's side, regarded Cassandra with seething anger. Varaminta and Poochie, both half-fainted on the ripped chair, were still recovering from their ordeal with Rameses, assisted by Dracula-Torquil.

'Alternatively, you can have an unlimited supply of ingredients,' Cassandra went on. 'As you say yourself, you've done quite handsomely out of just one. I'm sure you can concoct all manner of fiction about the others. So which is it to be, Omar; the recipe book...or the ingredients?'

Roman looked at the book, then at Cassandra; a muscle flickered in his cheek. 'There is another way, of course,' he said at last. 'I could just make copies—'

'Don't waste your time,' said Lulu. 'It can't be copied.'

'Built-in protection from the likes of you, *Omar*,' added Cassandra.

'My name is Roman!' said Roman Fisher through clenched teeth. Sausage Hands was so wound up by now, he had turned cross-eyed.

Roman paused. Then an oily smile spread across his face. 'You're right,' he said at last. 'We should let the child have her little plaything back...it isn't important.' Lulu noticed him exchange a glance with Varaminta. He spread his hands. 'Please!' he offered smarmily, 'give the book back, by all means.'

'You won't get a word out of me until I *know* the girls and the book are home safe,' Cassandra warned.

Roman's cheek twitched. 'Of course.' He was cornered. Lulu could tell he had no intention of carrying out Cassandra's wishes; he thought he could get away with just pretending to.

But Cassandra, of course, was smarter than that. '…And the only way I can be sure,' she added, 'is if I'm allowed to go along and see for myself.'

Varaminta snorted indignantly. 'Roman, you can't possibly—'

She was interrupted by Sausage Hands, who had finally burst and now lunged for Cassandra, grabbing *The Apple Star* with one giant mitt while simultaneously clamping the other around her upper body.

'No, you idiot!' shrieked Roman, jumping up and down, his watch chain jangling.

But the guard held firm, and while Cassandra struggled in his grip, Rameses attacked his ankle, and the commotion upset Poochie all over again.

'Oh my God, stop!' cried Varaminta, jumping up. 'My baby can't take it!' Poochie was trembling violently in her hands, its yappings now reduced to a squeaky warble. 'His little heart…I don't have his medicine!' Varaminta went on. 'This is an emergency – he needs a vet, *now*!' Clinging to the doglet, she trotted along the short stretch of canal towpath to the big gate. 'Somebody open this up!' she yelled, banging on it, and seconds later it began to crank its way open.

'*Ararararow, ararararow!*' went the traumatised Poochie.

An almighty *thud!* took Lulu by surprise: she turned and saw Sausage Hands flat on his face, apparently toppled by Torquil at this opportune moment, freeing once again both Cassandra and *The Apple Star*, and now Torquil, book in hand, was making a dash for the gate.

'Get him!' ordered Roman Fisher, and Lulu and Frenchy were suddenly released as all hands went for Torquil, Cassandra and *The Apple Star*. Within seconds everyone was running out towards the lock.

Up the stone steps, and through a narrow passageway...Lulu took great rasping gulps of the fresh night air as she ran, now entering a large marina. Tell Dad where you are, she reminded herself...*big marina*, she kept saying in her mind, *we've gone above ground into the big marina by the Thames*.

And all the time running, running...Torquil was still way ahead, followed by two of the guards. 'Torquil...won't know...how to get the ingredients!' Lulu panted to Frenchy. 'What is he *thinking*?'

'I don't know...the Psychic Psours have worn off,' Frenchy panted back.

'Oh, I didn't mean—'

'But it figures,' Frenchy went on, as they rounded the edge of the marina. 'He's so greedy...he doesn't want to share with Roman. He probably...reckons he'll be able to...find suppliers himself somehow!'

Don't know how, thought Lulu. But then she realised that Torquil wasn't the sort of person to let such details get in his way...

Lulu noticed that the talking was slowing them down, and thrust herself forward, her chest heaving with effort; Frenchy did likewise. Now they had completed the semicircle around the marina and were looking down on the massive gates of the great tidal lock that served as its entrance. Beyond them yawned a deep canyon which opened out into the black, glitter-edged expanse of the Thames. Lulu and Frenchy were gaining on the others; Cassandra and Roman were not far behind, while Varaminta was bringing up the rear, apparently having made her call to the vet.

They followed the road as it crossed over the canyon, then headed down a narrow street. Up ahead, Lulu saw Torquil suddenly dive into an alleyway on the left, but following him around the corner she found that it led straight back out to a sheer drop into the river. Torquil, having made the same discovery, panicked and rounded back, left with no alternative but to confront the enemy. He hurtled at the two guards straight as an arrow, roaring like a Samurai warrior – *oof!* went Sausage Hands, but managed to grab him and now a full on, free-for-all fight began.

In the confusion *The Apple Star* tumbled to the ground; not caring if her hand was crushed, Lulu instinctively reached in among the thundering boots for the little yellow book…seizing it, she gathered her skirts and hurtled back down the cobbled alleyway. 'Big marina!' she cried aloud now,' oh *please*, Dad, find me now!'

Got to *stay close* to the marina, she told herself – how else would he stand a chance? Oh Dad, Dad, where are you? she thought as she rushed around the corner and back along the narrow street, retracing her steps. Her knuckles dug into her chest as she clutched her precious book to her heart with her grimy fingers. But just as she was approaching the bridge over the lock Roman Fisher appeared, blocking her way; gasping, Lulu turned and dashed to the right – the only way she could go other than back into the hands of the guards. But this route took her along the edge of the castle-high walls of the marina entrance; the slooshing sound of water through sluice-gates filled her swimming head as she realised there was nothing between her and a four-storey drop into the Thames. Forcing herself not to look down, Lulu continued around the bend. What she saw amazed and delighted her; Dad and Aileen were running towards her.

'Dad!' she cried, then was jolted back as Roman Fisher clamped a surprisingly strong arm across her shoulders, and began dragging her closer to the precipice. 'Help!' she screamed, struggling to free herself.

'Let it go!' urged Roman, trying to prise *The Apple Star* free with his other hand.

But Lulu clung on to the book with all her might, at the same time frantically kicking this way and that. Then another arm was around her waist and Lulu realised it was Dad's; he and Roman were pulling her in different directions. Lulu saw the veins bulging on her father's temple as he tugged her away from the edge. His grip was firm, but so was Roman Fisher's, and Dad would not dare let go of Lulu to tackle him. And Dad was concentrating on saving Lulu, while all Roman cared about was *The Apple Star*; Lulu squealed as he gradually peeled her fingers away from the book...

Suddenly, there was a *thwack!* followed by a violent jolt and a loud moan as someone – yes, Aileen! – punched Roman in the face, but this dislodged his hand, bringing Lulu's hand with it, and before she knew what had happened Lulu had lost her grip of *The Apple Star*.

'No!' she cried as the precious book with its

inscription, *For my lovely Lulu, Happy Birthday, lots of love, Mum* went sailing through the air. It plummeted, pages flapping, down into the chasm below, and was swallowed by the choppy black waters of the river Thames.

Limehouse Arrest

Time stood still. The river kept right on plopping against the harbour wall, as if nothing had happened. A tiny light travelled sedately across the sky; an aeroplane on its way to some distant place, hurtling through the air like a shooting star. That star would soon return; *The Apple Star* would not. 'It's gone…' was all Lulu could say. She thought of her garden full of magical plants, her no-longer-secret supply of ingredients; what use was any of it now, if she had no idea how to put them all together? It would be like trying to assemble a jigsaw with pieces from different puzzles.

Gradually, a screaming in the air grew louder; Lulu thought her ears were ringing, until she realised it was the whine of police sirens. Dad gently pulled her away from the edge, saying, 'It's OK…everything's OK.'

No, it's not, thought Lulu, as she allowed herself to be led to safety. Aileen tried to comfort her too, but she felt numb. Her mind was a jumble as she tried to recollect just one instruction from a single recipe; it was all a blur. And even if she could remember anything, it would only disappear the moment she tried to write any of it down. It was hopeless, hopeless...

Still at the precipice stood Roman Fisher, his mouth contorted into an exaggerated downward curve like a theatrical mask. He too was saturated with grief, all dreams of his Roman empire dissolved forever. Then suddenly he snapped out of his daze and turned on Aileen. 'You stupid woman, just look what you've gone and done!' Furious, he lunged for her.

'Look out!' cried Dad, and quick as a flash Aileen rolled out of the way, flipped around and kicked back at Roman, sending him tottering backwards in his shiny shoes, right into the path of several police officers as they appeared around the bend. Two of them grabbed the elf king firmly by his pin-striped sleeves.

Dad gazed after her, so stunned he forgot to push his hair out of his eyes. 'Wow!' he breathed, then rushed forward to help Aileen to her feet. 'Hey, are you all right?'

'Yeah, no worries!' said Aileen nonchalantly, though Lulu could see she was shaking as she dusted herself down.

'Thank you, miss,' said one of the policemen. 'This one nearly got away.'

'I not do nothing!' protested Roman Fisher, suddenly reverting to a heavily accented voice instead of the refined 'English gentleman' act he'd been using up to now. Lulu stared at him in disbelief.

Lulu, Dad and Aileen followed the police and Roman Fisher back to the group that was gathered beside the lock. Frenchy and Cassandra looked on as Roman's guards, Varaminta and Torquil, assembled in a line by some other police officers, were having their rights read to them. A van with the words 'Pet Ambulance' on its side stood nearby, at the back of which Poochie was being treated to five-star emergency medical care.

'Varaminta!' gasped Lulu's dad. 'What are you doing here? What on earth is going on?'

'I demand to speak to my lawyer!' insisted the dishevelled Varaminta, her voice trembling. 'Oh my poor baby!' she added, gazing in the direction of her traumatised doglet.

Lulu looked nervously at Cassandra. Would she let on to the police about *The Apple Star*? Surely not; she would know better than to expose Lulu to such scrutiny – especially since whatever happened now would be all over the news tomorrow.

Then Cassandra caught Lulu's eye and winked, and Lulu knew her secret was safe. Desperate as she was about losing the precious magical book itself, this wonderful legacy she had inherited that now languished in the mud at the bottom of the Thames, she nevertheless did not relish the prospect of explaining all about it to the police.

A policewoman clamped handcuffs on Roman Fisher. 'This big misunderstanding,' he insisted, still using his fake accent. 'I just try stop these people fight. I no want any trouble, I just here on holiday.'

Cassandra turned to him in amazement. 'Oh really, Roman Fisher? So who is it that runs Roman Fisher Enterprises, then?'

oman gave her a quizzical look. 'I not know what she mean. I Omar Rishnef, come from Morocco. I on holiday, see Big Ben, London Eye. I no want trouble.'

Lulu was aghast. He wouldn't get away with this, surely?

'You'll have plenty of time to explain yourself down at the station, sir,' said the officer in charge. Next, he turned to Varaminta, 'As for this one; a right little wildcat you are, aren't you?'

'I'll say she is,' said the policewoman, rubbing her head. 'You should see the bump I've got where she whacked me with her stiletto!'

The policeman gave a sharp intake of breath. 'Nasty,' he remarked. He turned to Varaminta. 'My mum's a big fan of yours, you know. Loves that show, *The Fashion Police*. How's it go? "I arrest you for crimes against fashion." You're her favourite. As for me – well, try coming round my place telling me how to live my life, I'll knock yer block off!' Then he turned to his bruised colleague, and rubbed his hands together with relish. 'D'you know, there's been times when I've been fed up with my job. All the pen-pushing an' that. Then a moment like this comes along, makes it all worthwhile. Know what I mean?'

'I certainly do,' said the policewoman.

Lulu noticed that the other officers were struggling to keep a straight face. They obviously knew *The Fashion Police* too, and were enjoying this very much indeed.

'Stiletto, eh?' said the policeman, taking out a pair of handcuffs. 'I think that calls for a special charge, don't you? So here goes: Varaminta le Bone, I arrest you on the charge of crimes *involving* fashion!'

There was a spontaneous round of applause from the other police officers. The policewoman smiled. 'Couldn't have put it better myself.'

Something Fishy

The camera zoomed in on the blonde woman in dark glasses, holding up her bag to conceal her face as she hurried into the back of a car.

'Speculation has been growing today over allegations made against the television celebrity Varaminta le Bone,' said the voice-over. 'The forty-two-year-old star of the popular TV show *The Fashion Police* was arrested late last night after being involved in a brawl in the Limehouse area of London. She was fined for assaulting a police officer; however, due to the circumstances of the fight it has been suggested that Miss le Bone may be subject to additional charges. There is controversy over the identity of another person involved in the fight. A fifty-four-year-old Moroccan man claiming to be a holiday-maker denies allegations that he is in fact a Mr Roman Fisher, head of an illegal trading company called Roman Fisher Enterprises. His claims are borne out by three friends—'

'His guards!' cried Lulu.

'Of course they'll back him up,' said Dad. 'It'd be more than their life was worth if they didn't, I'll bet!'

'…However, the whereabouts of Mr Fisher himself have yet to be established,' the newscaster went on. 'Miss le Bone denies any connection to either individual, and she and the Moroccan have been released on bail pending further inquiries.'

'Released on bail!' cried Aileen. 'They ought to lock 'em up and throw away the key!'

Dad switched the TV off. 'I dare say Varaminta can afford expensive lawyers,' he said dismissively. He put his arm around Lulu. 'And as for that other character – well, he's a nasty piece of work and should be put away—'

'Yes, Dad, but we *know* why we don't want to press charges, don't we?' Lulu reminded him pointedly.

Dad sighed. 'Yes, yes…well, at least we know he's no threat to you any more. I'm just glad you're home safe.'

'Thanks to you,' said Lulu.

'I couldn't have done it without those green sweets,' said Dad. 'Noodle, you're a genius, I swear! I really am very proud of you.'

Lulu looked at him sheepishly. 'You're not angry with me for going off like that, then?'

'No!' said Dad. 'Still a bit shocked, but not angry.'

Since the events of last night, everything was now out in the open about exactly what was going on in the garden with all those strange plants, and Lulu's attic supply of magical ingredients. Dad knew that he owed his lustrous new head of hair to one of Lulu's recipes. He knew that those strange nugget things she'd been cooking up every morning for a week had been to help someone at school who was suffering from bullying. And of course, Lulu had explained all about the Psychic Psours and Medium Sweets. What they hadn't discussed was whether a magical recipe had been behind those extraordinary outpourings of ugly truths of Torquil's last summer, which had led to Dad's break-up with Varaminta. Nor did Lulu have any idea whether Dad knew that she had tried to pair him off with Frenchy's mum, using the Cupid Cakes. If he did, he was very kindly not mentioning it.

And then there was *The Apple Star*. Dad had, of course, demanded an explanation as to what Lulu had been doing halfway across town, late at night, being pursued by a bunch of thugs, when she had told him she was at a Halloween party. And so, of course, Lulu had explained the whole thing. About how *The Apple Star* had come to her in the first place, and how it seemed to be from Mum – Dad had become quite dewy-eyed at this part – about the fact that it had been stolen, and she and Frenchy had been trying to get it back. And now it was gone.

'You know, I hate to say this,' said Dad, 'but—'

'But perhaps it's just as well it's at the bottom of the Thames,' Lulu finished his sentence for him. 'That's what you were going to say, wasn't it?'

'I know that's not what you want to hear right now,' said Dad. 'But it's the way I feel...I don't ever want you to be in that kind of danger again.'

Lulu lowered her eyes; 'I wish you'd seen it now.' On the other hand, she thought, perhaps it was best he hadn't...not with those Truth Cookie and Cupid Cake recipes in there! But the part of her that believed it really was a magical gift from Mum wished she could have let Dad in on the secret.

'And you say that gardener was really Grodmila in disguise?' said Dad.

'Yes,' said Lulu. 'She stole *The Apple Star*, I'm sure of it.'

Dad groaned and put his face in his hands. 'Oh no...that explains a lot. Costas was just saying the other day how he couldn't understand where "Andreas" had got to. Said he had regularly played backgammon with him at his local bar...Andreas was a good player, he said, although very quiet. But then he had disappeared, and when Costas tried to call him, the line was dead. Good grief, I've got to be more careful in future…I just assumed they were old pals!'

'It's not your fault, Dad,' said Lulu, feeling heavier than ever.

Upstairs in her room, Lulu took the picture of Mum-in-Muddy-Wellies off the bedside table. 'I just can't believe it's gone,' she found herself saying. 'What did it all mean, Mum?' Tears welled up in her eyes. 'What was the point of it all? What am I now?'

The Quicksilver Tree

Lulu sat quietly by herself and watched Dad help prepare the bonfire for lighting. She usually enjoyed the annual school Guy Fawkes Night party, but tonight she wasn't in a sociable mood. From Mrs Pye's dreary lessons, no longer enlivened by the Upside-Down Cake, to Zena Lemon, who had found someone new to pick on, everything seemed a cruel reminder of what she had lost. And soon she would be losing Aileen too, thanks to the Chocolate Wishes.

The bonfire burst into flames. The guy, perched on top in its baggy old second-hand suit, reminded her curiously of Roman Fisher. Even its face, a Halloween devil mask, looked a bit like him.

'Hello, Lulu,' said a familiar deep voice.

Lulu jumped up in surprise. 'Cassandra! What are you doing here?'

'I came to see you, of course,' said Cassandra, sitting down next to Lulu. She glanced around.

'Sometimes busy places offer the most privacy.'

'Are you...being watched?' asked Lulu.

'Omar's still a free man,' Cassandra reminded her. 'And I still have what he wants, so I must leave England for good.'

'Oh no, you can't!' cried Lulu.

'I must. But I wanted to see you first. I know how you must be feeling about *The Apple Star*, and I wanted to remind you of what you still have.'

'What's that?'

A distant firework lit up the sky, spilling out its sparkling trail like the birth of the Milky Way. 'Your star!' said Cassandra. 'Remember? The one that speaks to you across time and space?'

'I don't know what use it is any more,' sighed Lulu, as she watched the swirling sparks of the bonfire drift higher into the black sky.

The fire was reflected in Cassandra's eyes. 'That purpose you found is not lost, I promise. Once you have it, it's yours forever – I know, it's the same with me.'

'What happened with Omar, Cassandra?' asked Lulu. 'How did he get to be so...' she trailed off, not knowing where to begin.

'Nasty? Greedy? I think he always was. Remember the story I told you about the shipwreck I foretold?'

'Yes.'

'I wonder if you can guess what sort of cargo that ship was carrying?'

Lulu frowned. Then it dawned on her. 'Oh! You mean—'

Cassandra smiled. 'Now you get it! The last survivor passed everything on to me; a box he was clutching which contained a cargo inventory and list of suppliers. He did that because I tried to rescue him. "Now you have come, the magical secret will live on," he kept saying; then he died.'

'What, you actually went to that island where the ship was wrecked?' asked Lulu.

Cassandra nodded. 'Believe it or not, that was Omar's idea; he got me to go ashore first, to prove we wouldn't be pecked to death by the falcons. But it turned out he didn't care about saving lives; all he was interested in was looting. He wouldn't even help when I found that survivor – not even when I told him about the "magical secret".'

'Well, I guess he's changed his mind about that now!' said Lulu.

'Yes,' said Cassandra. 'Some years ago, actually. But it took him a long time to track me down... he went to prison for seven years after trying to sell the valuables he'd plundered from the shipwreck. And he had found some real gems, although of course he didn't let on to me at the time; that's why he didn't care about the "magical secret". But by the time he came out of prison he felt very differently. I had already moved to London, making sure no one told him where I had gone. That's when he went back to Falcon Island, to see what he could discover for himself.'

'Oh, would that be "the secret island where money grows on trees"?' asked Lulu, remembering Roman Fisher's sarcastic explanation of where he'd got the Quicksilver berries.

'That's right,' said Cassandra. 'The Quicksilver tree loves a harsh landscape; rocks, high winds. The seeds had sown themselves where almost nothing else would, and after seven years the trees had grown to maturity. You know, a Quicksilver tree with ripe berries glistening in the sun really does look as if it were laden with coins. Which, it seems, was the beginning of Omar's big idea.'

'The Midas Touch.'

'Exactly. But eventually he wanted more; if this was just one part of the "magical secret" what other wonders were there for him yet to discover? That's when he became determined to track me down. And now he has. He knew, too, about a magical recipe book…he thought I would have that, or know someone who did.'

'But surely he'll be found out before long,' said Lulu. 'And then he'll be back in prison.'

'How?' asked Cassandra. 'That identity – Omar Rishnef – is his true one. And he has plenty of people to back him up; he's a seasoned crook now, and he had this all planned in case he ever got caught. Of course, the police have closed down Roman Fisher Enterprises, and confiscated everything there; not only were his claims for "The Midas Touch" obviously fraudulent, he also doesn't pay his taxes. But all he'll do is spring up somewhere else, in some other guise. He's like the Hydra; cut off one head, and three more will grow in its place. That's why I must leave. But please don't forget what I said about your gift; I really do believe that in some shape or form, it is yours forever...have *faith*, my child!' Cassandra squeezed Lulu's hand, then wafted away, her robes billowing behind her.

Lulu remained, staring at the bonfire as she tried to make sense of all Cassandra had said. Her reference to the Hydra reminded her of a picture in her favourite book, *The Twelve Labours of Heracles*. As she gazed into the flames, the burning branches became those used by Heracles as he seared the severed roots of the Hydra's many heads to prevent them from multiplying. There *has* to be some way I can help Cassandra, she thought...

Dolly Mixture

Chocolate éclairs. Those might cheer me up a bit, thought Lulu as she chose the packet of sweets from the array in the newsagent's. She loved the way the hard toffee outside of the candies melted away in the mouth, releasing the chocolatey inside. There was something comforting about that – and right now, with so much slipping away from her, Lulu needed all the comfort she could get. Cassandra was leaving the country, and Aileen would be moving out today...and soon would be gone for good.

Lulu turned, and was confronted with the Sunday paper headlines. *FASHION POLICE STAR IS GANGSTER'S MOLL* screamed one of the tabloids; **VARAMINTA'S SECRET UNDERWORLD LIFE OF CRIME** yelled another, all accompanied by grainy paparazzi pictures of Varaminta leaving her house. Lulu checked her purse to see how much money she had, then swiped up three of the papers and put them on the counter next to the chocolate éclairs.

Lulu knew Dad wouldn't approve, so when she got home she smuggled the papers straight up to her room. The headlines had surprised her; she was sure Varaminta had not been found guilty of anything other than the incident with the policewoman. Even when she read the stories, it was hard to see what the reporters were basing them on. But they were certainly having fun doing it, and the more Lulu read, the clearer it became that Varaminta's once adoring audience was turning against her. It didn't seem to matter to anyone, journalist or viewer, whether there was truth in any of the rumours; the rumours themselves had emerged genie-like from the lamp of reality, and taken on a life of their own. And here they were, in full vulgar tabloid colour, granting the wishes of the readers, because the readers had decided they now hated Varaminta le Bone. **READERS' POLL: Should she stay or should she go? 70% say she should GO!!'**

'Well, I'd love to stay, but I gotta go,' came Aileen's voice from the doorway.

Lulu hurriedly shoved the papers together and sat on them.

'Don't be embarrassed, kiddo!' said Aileen, coming in and shutting the door. 'I've been reading that stuff myself. Isn't it brilliant? I tell ya, Varaminta's expensive lawyers can whitewash all they like, but they can't control public opinion. You poms have always done a thorough job of public humiliation; you'll soon finish her off, just wait and see!'

Lulu gave a rueful smile. 'Too bad we can't do the same to the Hydra.'

'What's that?'

'Oh, nothing.'

'Well, come and say goodbye to Dolly,' said Aileen.

Lulu helped Aileen down the stairs with some of her things, and they watched Dad as he carefully carried Dolly the mannequin. 'You men, you're all the same,' joked Aileen. 'No sooner does a girl come into your life than you boot her out!'

Dad tripped on the bottom stair and lunged forward to regain his balance, colliding with Aileen.

'Whoops!' said Aileen.

'S-sorry,' said Dad, as he fumbled with Dolly, trying to straighten the coat that was falling off her shoulder. He accidentally grabbed Aileen's hand as she, too, tried to adjust the coat, then withdrew it, embarrassed. His hair flopped in front of his eyes, and he smoothed it back. 'Sorry,' he said again, then, 'Well!'

'Well!' echoed Aileen. 'I'll be off, then.' She turned to Lulu. 'Seeya, kid!'

Lulu stepped forward and gave her a quick hug. 'Bye. It's been cool having you around. Hasn't it, Dad?'

Lulu thought Dad seemed a little flustered about something. 'Y-yes,' he stammered, apparently not knowing where to look. Then he gave Aileen a bright, cheery smile and added, 'Really...uh, *cool*.' He cleared his throat. 'Anyway. Still a few more weeks before you're gone for good, isn't it?'

'You interviewed anyone for my replacement yet, Michael?' asked Aileen.

Dad seemed taken off guard. 'Your *replacement*? Ah, yes, that...well...'

'Better get a move-on, y'know!' said Aileen. 'Not much time left.'

'No...no, I suppose not,' said Dad. Lulu thought he looked the way she felt.

*

The Apple Star. Aileen. Cassandra.

Three beacons of light in Lulu's life, all disappearing into the ether, leaving Lulu feeling lonelier than ever. She picked up the newspapers from that morning and shoved them in the waste-paper bin, no longer feeling very triumphant over the decline of Varaminta's career. Even that couldn't compensate for all she was losing – or the fact that the newer, more dangerous enemy, Roman Fisher, was still on the loose, soon to be sprouting Hydra-like in new directions. She had noticed a mention in one of the papers that he was due to appear in court in a week's time, but that was only to do with the street fight; no doubt nothing else would come of it.

She threw herself onto her bed and gazed up out of the skylight, remembering Cassandra's words: 'You still have your star'. Lulu so wanted to be comforted by this, but it didn't seem to be happening for her. She reminded herself also of Cassandra's mysterious reference to her 'gift', which she still supposedly had, 'in some shape or form' – whatever that meant.

It was only six o'clock, but already the sky was dark. Not knowing what else to do, Lulu looked for her star, as a focus for her thoughts. Having located it, she found herself thinking about the moment when Roman Fisher had transformed himself back into Omar Rishnef before their very eyes. The way Lulu had felt just then was, she realised now, a very familiar sensation; she had felt it countless times when Varaminta and Torquil were around, constantly distorting the truth to suit their own ends. And now here was another deceiver, busily making Cassandra's life a misery; so much so, it was forcing her out of the country.

'If only we had those Truth Cookies now!' Lulu found herself saying aloud, quite surprising herself.

It was at this moment that a realisation dawned on Lulu that was so fantastic, so utterly brilliant, she knew she must tell Cassandra about it urgently. Cursing the loss of her mobile phone, she almost fell over as she threw herself across the room to get to her desk. Somewhere...*somewhere* she still had that business card Cassandra had given her the first time they'd met. It wasn't until she'd turned practically everything upside-down that she remembered: inside the cover of *The Twelve Labours of Heracles*.

She had to call twice, leaving a voicemail message the first time; Cassandra was screening calls. 'Thank God I've reached you!' Lulu almost shouted when at last Cassandra answered. 'Listen, you're not to go anywhere, you understand? I've discovered something wonderful and amazing and you've got to promise me you'll stay for at least a week!'

Baker's Dozen

'OK, where's the fire?' asked Frenchy, as she appeared on the doorstep.

Lulu pulled her in and shut the door. She glanced towards the living room, where Dad was. 'Tell you upstairs!' she whispered.

'OK, but I haven't got long, Lu! Mum's been keeping close tabs on me ever since Halloween.'

Upstairs in her room, Lulu was virtually splitting at the seams with excitement. She tapped her finger to her temple. 'French, it's all up here! Every last word of it!'

Frenchy blinked at her. 'What is? Oh! You mean—'

Lulu grabbed her by the arms. 'My *recipes*, French! All the ones I've made, and all in the minutest detail...every exact measurement, every instruction, I can remember it all!'

Frenchy's jaw dropped. 'What – not the whole book?'

'Huh? Oh, no...only the ones I've actually *made*. But isn't that amazing?'

'Oh Lu, that's totally brilliant!'

'She *told* me I still had it – Cassandra, that is; "you still have your gift",' Lulu went on, imitating Cassandra's deep voice. '"In some shape or form, it is yours forever." I didn't understand what she meant, not until today. In fact at first it seemed as if I'd forgotten *everything*. It wasn't until I calmed down and focused on my star that it all came flooding back!'

'Amazing,' said Frenchy. She cocked her head to one side. 'And...you don't want your dad to know?'

'Oh!' sighed Lulu. 'I don't know – I haven't figured out that part yet. All I know is, when I discovered this I just needed to tell you as soon as possible!'

'How many recipes *have* you made, by the way?'

Lulu hopped over to her desk and picked up a scrap of paper. 'I made a list; there's twelve of them!' She handed the list to Frenchy:

1 Truth Cookies
2 Cupid Cakes
3 Candy-Coated Anti-Dote
4 Nuggets of Information
5 Psychic Psours, Medium Sweets (count as one)
6 Chocolate Wishes
7 Fuzzbooster Flapjacks
8 Mighty Muffins
9 Sharp-Eye Shake
10 Upside-Down Cake
11 Hush Brownies
12 Sandman Smoothie

Frenchy gasped. 'Oh boy!' she cried. 'Lulu Baker's dozen!'

'Oh yeah,' said Lulu. 'You're right. Ha ha! Hey, isn't a baker's dozen thirteen?'

'Well, number five is sort of like two recipes, isn't it?'

'I guess so...Lulu Baker's Dozen!' Lulu repeated. 'They're *my* recipes, French! Now no one can take them away from me – not Varaminta, nor Torquil or Grodmila...not even that Roman Fisher crook!'

Frenchy sat down on the bed, still staring at the list. 'Lu, this is so fantastic. Hey, you don't even need *The Apple Star* any more! These were the recipes you were meant to have. You *chose* them, like – I don't know, like they're your three wishes, only quadrupled.'

Lulu sat beside her and looked at the list. 'You're right...it's quite a bunch to have, isn't it?'

'Incredible,' agreed Frenchy. 'Trust me, you really couldn't wish for better.'

'Funny how it worked out that I've got six Level Three, or "extreme" recipes, and six Level One, or "mild" ones. I divided them into columns; extreme on the left, mild on the right.'

'Oh yeah...but Lu, what about the ingredients?

What's happening with Cassandra?'

Lulu smiled. 'French, we've got a plan...'

*

The orange cookies looked and smelled just as delicious as they had the first time Lulu had made them. A lovely Halloween pumpkin colour, with a rich, nutty aroma. Truth Cookies.

It turned out there were just two ingredients that Lulu didn't have in her store: crow's eggs and camel butter. But even though Cassandra had lost all the supplies Roman Fisher had plundered, she still knew where to get more, and in five days the order had arrived.

There were also two other things Lulu had needed from Cassandra, and since Roman didn't steal them, not realising they were anything to do with the making of magical recipes, Cassandra still had them. They were an ostrich feather, and some special ink. The ostrich feather, symbol of Ma'at, the ancient Egyptian goddess of truth, was needed for some incantations. The ink was for the 'Reasons'; Lulu had to write on a piece of paper the reasons these particular Truth Cookies were being made, then immerse the paper in water and add the resulting infusion to the recipe. When it came to the moment when all the ingredients were mixed together, she even knew to stand back while it bubbled up, and not to return to the bowl until the final big, hot bubble was expelled. Last time she had gone back too soon, and been left with a spot of 'sunburn' which hadn't been easy to explain away. And there was one other special instruction; Cassandra had asked Lulu to make the cookies smaller, and almond-shaped.

'Why?' asked Lulu.

'All will become clear,' said Cassandra.

Dad had come into the kitchen when Lulu was making them. 'Oh Noodle,' he'd said. 'I'm so glad you're still cooking. I was worried you might have gone off it, after what happened with…that book.' Of course, he had no idea that Lulu was making one of its magical recipes.

And now the day had arrived: Roman Fisher's court hearing. Lulu had worried about how to get him to eat the cookies, but Cassandra had reassured her, saying, 'Just hand them to me, and I'll do the rest!'

After some dispute, Dad had agreed to take Lulu and Frenchy to the hearing. 'It's not a *trial*, you know,' he'd protested. 'It'll probably be over in five minutes.'

'All the more reason why it's not a big deal,' Lulu had countered, and Dad had relented. He was, however, most irritated when the hearing was delayed by nearly an hour. He kept muttering under his breath about having work to do, and disappearing outside to make phone calls.

While he was out, Cassandra returned to the dingy waiting room and sat down serenely next to Lulu, having disposed of the cookies.

'There's been a delay,' Frenchy told her.

'Oh, good!' beamed Cassandra. Then she whispered to Lulu, 'The hungrier Roman gets, the better!'

Lulu looked around the room, and furtively whispered back, 'How did you do it?'

Cassandra smiled. 'Omar's, ahem, *favourite aunt* sent him some home-made cookies: little almond-shaped ones, like she's always made.'

Lulu's eyes widened. 'Your mum?' she mouthed.

Cassandra nodded, her shoulders going up and down as she chuckled silently. 'She even enclosed a note in Arabic, forgiving him for his past sins.'

*

'...And the plaintiff denies these charges, is that correct?' said the judge.

'That is correct, your honour,' replied the policeman, the same one who had arrested Roman Fisher on Halloween night.

The judge, a sharp-suited woman with silver hair, gave a wry smile. 'Even though it's obvious that "Roman Fisher" is an anagram of "Omar Rishnef".'

The man sitting next to Omar/Roman, apparently his lawyer, jumped to his feet. 'With respect, your honour, that *coincidence* proves nothing whatsoever, and—'

'Yes, of course, I know,' interrupted the judge, waving her hand wearily at him. 'Oh, *do* sit down!'

The lawyer, an oily-looking man with dandruff, reluctantly returned to his seat. Lulu leaned forward to get a closer look at Roman Fisher. Something about the tightness of his lips, the furrowed brow, suggested he was indeed straining to control the urge to blurt out the truth. Any minute now…

'So this mysterious Mr Fisher still hasn't been tracked down?' asked the judge.

'We're still working on that, your honour,' admitted the policeman.

Suddenly, Roman Fisher stood up. All eyes turned to him. 'It's me!' he cried.

Yes! thought Lulu; she noticed he had that same shocked expression as Torquil had when the Truth Cookies had made him spill the beans.

The lawyer looked aghast. He tugged at Roman's sleeve, trying to pull him back into his seat. 'Your honour, I—'

'Let him speak!' snapped the judge. She turned to Roman. 'You were saying...?'

'It's no coincidence about the names,' he declared boldly, his voice returning to its 'English gentleman' accent. 'I *am* Roman Fisher!'

There were mutterings all around the courtroom. Roman's lawyer put his face in his hands.

The judge raised her eyebrows. 'Well, that was easy, wasn't it?' She took up her spectacles, which hung on a chain around her neck, and put them on. 'Let me see now...'

'I am Roman Fisher, that's right!' Roman went on, unable to stop now. 'I'm a crook, and a brilliant one!' he declared at the top of his voice.

His lawyer had rolled forward and was slowly knocking his forehead on his desk.

Bang! went the judge's gavel. 'Brilliant or not, you're going to prison, Roman Fisher!'

Lulu beamed at Cassandra, who gave her a discreet little thumbs-up sign.

Frenchy squeezed Lulu's arm. 'You did it!' she whispered excitedly.

Food of the Gods

Lulu placed three Chocolate Wishes in the middle of each square of shimmery purple silk she had laid out on the kitchen table. She tied them up with silver ribbons, and brought them through to the living room on a tray.

Aileen was on her knees by the fireplace, fixing a special Christmas mantelpiece arrangement she had made, a mix of green and silver foliage and illuminated stars.

'Oh, Dad's going to love that!' said Lulu.

Aileen sat back on her heels. 'I hope so. Goes well with the tree, doesn't it?' Lulu usually decorated the Christmas tree herself, bringing out the same old tired baubles year after year. But this time it was a splendid creation in forest green, purple and silver, courtesy of Aileen.

'I *love* the tree,' said Lulu, as she began tying her little bags of chocolates to it. There were to be twelve friends and family members on Christmas day, and each of them – including Lulu herself – would get three Chocolate Wishes. Lulu couldn't help feeling sad that Aileen, who was going home to Australia for Christmas, wouldn't be one of them. In fact, this was her very last day of being employed by Lulu's dad; in January, she would start her exciting new job, and Lulu would no longer have her around as friend, big sister, favourite aunt. Tonight they were going out for dinner to mark the occasion.

Lulu heard the front door open and close; Dad was home. 'Ooh, quick!' said Aileen, jumping to her feet and pulling the scrunchy from her hair. She dived for the power switch, and just as Dad entered the room, the tree lit up. 'Ta-da!' said Aileen.

Dad stopped dead in his tracks and blinked. 'Wow!' He went over to admire the fireplace. 'Did you do all this, Aileen?'

Aileen shrugged modestly. 'Yeah, it's…just a sort of farewell present.'

'D'you like it, then?' asked Lulu.

'It's great,' said Dad, his voice now tinged with sadness. 'That's a nice dress you've got on too,' he added, noting the effort Aileen had made for their night out. 'Don't often see you in a…in a dress. Nice, um, thing with the…' he gestured, indicating the trimming on the neckline.

'Thanks!' said Aileen, colouring slightly. There was an awkward silence. 'Well!' she said brightly.

'Well!' said Dad.

'Are we going then?' asked Lulu.

Dad ran his fingers through his luxuriant head of hair. 'Er...yup.'

*

Lulu liked to call him Willy Wonka – although that wasn't his real last name, of course. But since he ran a restaurant on the top floor of an old chocolate factory, which was even *called* 'The Chocolate Factory', and since he was a loud and ebullient character with apple cheeks and caterpillar eyebrows, it suited him wonderfully.

'MIKE, my old friend, NOW we can talk!' boomed Willy towards the end of the meal as the restaurant began to empty out. He put a bottle of brandy on the table and sat down to join them. 'Did you hear the latest news?' he said, pouring a drink for Lulu's dad. 'I see that Varaminta woman's lost her job with *The Fashion Police*.'

'Whoo!' cried Aileen rather loudly, slapping the table and prompting the people at the next table to stare at her.

Dad looked startled for a moment, then burst out laughing. This set Lulu off giggling, and finally Aileen as well.

Willy raised his furry eyebrows. 'Well! Sounds like cause for celebration. Cheers!' He raised his glass.

'Hic!' went Aileen. 'Oh no!' she said. 'I mustn't laugh, I'll *hic!* – oh, strewth!'

'Have a glass of water,' said Lulu's dad, pouring her one. Aileen drank, but her hiccups just got worse.

'You're supposed to drink it *upside down*!' insisted Lulu, still giggling. 'Pretend you're in Australia already.'

'How about some fresh air?' suggested Willy. 'Why don't you go out on the terrace?'

'*Hic!* That sounds like a *hic!* good idea,' said Aileen, getting up to go. ''Scuse me!'

'She loved your food, Willy,' remarked Dad, after she'd left. 'Must've eaten it a bit too fast.'

'Oh, I *do* like a woman who enjoys her food!' beamed Willy, cheeks aglow.

Dad glanced at Aileen on the terrace. 'Oh look, she'll freeze – she didn't take her coat,' he said, getting up. 'Be right back.' And off he went with Aileen's coat.

'Ah, the age of chivalry is not yet dead!' sighed Willy. He turned to Lulu. 'How's your chocolate pud?'

'I'm eating it r-e-a-l-l-y s-l-o-w-l-y, because it's so good,' said Lulu. And because I don't want this evening to end, she thought, though she didn't say that. For when it did, that would mean the end of Aileen's last day...

'I think your friend Aileen could take a leaf out of your book!' joked Willy.

Lulu smiled at his choice of words. 'I guess so.' My book, she thought wistfully, fondly remembering *The Apple Star*. But although she missed it, she was no longer filled with that desperate, longing sadness over its loss – not now that she had her very own Baker's Dozen of recipes permanently lodged in her memory. In fact if anything, she realised it had been quite a burden; now she was free of all that anxiety over having it stolen from her. Losing Aileen, however, did make her feel sad. How she would miss her!

'...Don't you think?' said Willy.

'I'm sorry?' said Lulu, suddenly realising she hadn't been listening to him.

'I said, you can pretend to be the gods on Mount Olympus up here,' Willy repeated. 'Eating ambrosia while you survey the mortals below!'

Lulu took another spoonful of her chocolate pudding, reminded of her magically enhanced geography lesson. 'Did you know that the scientific name for chocolate actually means "food of the gods"?'

Willy beamed. 'Quite right too!'

How appropriate, thought Lulu, that it should have been chocolates she had given Aileen, which allowed her to scale new heights in her life. Taking another mouthful of chocolate pudding, she glanced out of the window onto the terrace. What she saw made her pudding start to go down the wrong way. She dropped her spoon and began coughing.

Willy looked alarmed. 'What is it?'

Lulu grabbed her napkin and coughed into it some more, turning away from the window. She didn't know whether to be embarrassed, or happy, or...she didn't know what to think. What she had seen was so unexpected: Dad kissing Aileen.

'Ah,' said Willy, apparently having noticed as well by now. 'Well, that's the best cure for hiccups I know of!' he quipped.

The Icing on the Cake

There's always cake involved somehow, thought Lulu. The cake was the focal point of a birthday party, just as it had been on her fifth, when her mum had made her a gigantic fairy-tale castle cake. Five candles glittering like stars atop its turrets, ready for little Lulu to blow them out and make a wish. What had she wished for? Lulu couldn't remember now; probably a pony.

Even when something terrible happened, cake happened too. Whether it was war, famine or natural disaster, there would be Lulu, baking something for a cake sale to raise money for aid. And in her small way, she had also helped people with recipes such as her Upside-Down Cake and Cupid Cakes.

And then there were weddings. Some people felt the need for cakes that scraped the ceiling, dazzling white Parthenons piled above each other, topped with a gazebo housing a mini replica of the happy couple. That's what Varaminta would have had...

But this one was not like that at all. A pale yellow ziggurat, topped with a still-life arrangement of icing shaped like apples and gleaming with gold leaf, invisible wire looping over the top, supporting a host of silver stars. There were just five people at the wedding who understood this tribute to *The Apple Star*: the bride, the groom, Frenchy, Cassandra...and of course Lulu herself. The day was significant too; it was now summer again, and today was exactly two years from the date that Dad was to have married Varaminta.

Only now he was marrying Aileen instead. Strewth! as Aileen would say. Who'd have thought it?

Frenchy and Glynnie joined Lulu and together they watched as the bride and groom cut the cake. There was a roar of applause, then the music struck up and Dad led Aileen to the floor for the first dance.

Across the table sat Aileen's parents; freckle-faced and crinkly-but-young, they beamed with pride. 'Ooh, she looks a picture!' exclaimed Aileen's mum, dabbing her eyes with her napkin. 'That's an old evening dress of mine, you know,' she told Lulu.

'Ah, brings back memories!' added Aileen's dad. 'D'you know, she wouldn't even *let* us buy her something new.'

'So *not* like the V-woman!' whispered Frenchy.

'Oh boy, you're not kidding,' agreed Lulu, remembering the metres and metres of duchesse satin Varaminta had ordered at vast expense, and the number of fittings she'd gone for. All in preparation for her big *Chow!* magazine wedding that had everything to do with Varaminta and nothing to do with Dad. 'Aileen couldn't care less about all that show-offy stuff,' she added. 'Actually, I think she's a lot like Mum in that way.' It wasn't until she had said it, that Lulu realised just how true this was. Mum always looked so mesmerisingly lovely in those old pictures, even when wearing some 'best' outfit that was a bit haphazard. Dressing up had never been her strong point; she was happier in wellies.

'Perhaps that's why your dad loves her,' said Glynnie.

Lulu watched as Dad and Aileen twirled across the dance floor; he with his youthful locks of hair, she with her quirky 1970's silk flounces. 'Yes, I really think he does.' She smiled as she thought about the way things had turned out; how in using the Chocolate Wishes to help Aileen achieve something that seemed to be completely against her own interests, Lulu herself had eventually been rewarded in such a delightfully unexpected way.

Whereas Varaminta, in fighting tooth and glossily-manicured nail to get her way, had ended up losing it all: Dad, *The Apple Star*...even her status as TV star seemed impossible to resurrect now. And Roman Fisher's greed had finally landed him in jail.

Aileen's mum peered at the floral arrangement. 'What unusual-looking flowers you have in England!' she remarked.

'My wife, she do,' said Costas, who was sitting nearby. 'Good, eh?' He winked at Lulu, who smiled back. The 'unusual-looking flowers' had come from her own garden, including the spectacular deep pink summer blossoms of the Idzumo tree. Fortunately the cut branches were unable to speak.

'You know, Lulu,' confided Costas, 'now I so used to them plants, I kinda likey them!'

'I'm glad, Costas,' said Lulu. 'They have ...*character*, don't they?'

Costas let out a loud throaty laugh. 'Character, yes!'

'Oh look,' said Frenchy, 'they're giving out the cake.'

Lulu jumped up. 'Great! I've been looking forward to this.'

Frenchy gave her a sideways look. 'Lu,' she whispered. 'You haven't...tampered with it, have you?'

Lulu gasped in mock horror, giving Frenchy

a playful shove. 'French! As if! Sometimes normal food has enough magic of its own, you know. Come on.'

As they went over, Lulu was reminded of her mum's words all those years ago, when Lulu was just five. Mum's face glowed in the light from the oven, where a cake swelled like a mother's belly. 'It's like magic, isn't it?' she'd said.

Yes, it certainly was.

The End

Have you read the first two books
in the Lulu Baker trilogy?

The
Truth
Cookie

Discover a magical recipe book that gives Lulu Baker the power to change lives...

Lulu's dad has a new love, Varaminta le Bone. She's a sizzling sensation...and pure poison. How can Lulu make her dad see Varaminta, and her odious son Torquil, for who they really are?

Then Lulu stumbles into an odd little bookshop and Ambrosia May's mysterious recipe book falls at her feet. *The Apple Star,* together with some *very* unusual ingredients, just might do the trick...

Cupid
Cakes

One bite and you're smitten!

Thanks to Lulu Baker and her magical recipe book, The Apple Star, romance is in the air!

Lulu and her best friend Frenchy are inspired by the school production of *A Midsummer Night's Dream* to play cupid to Lulu's dad and...Frenchy's mum! But no sooner has Lulu whipped up the recipe for Cupid Cakes, and given Dad a taster – disaster strikes. It soon seems like everyone is falling in love with the wrong person!

And there is something deeper and darker worrying Lulu. Evil Varaminta le Bone and her tricksy son Torquil are back! Varaminta has uncovered the magical powers of *The Apple Star* and now she'll stop at nothing to get her hands on the book...

And don't miss

The Silk Sisters

trilogy,
also by Fiona Dunbar!

*Dressing up has never been
such an adventure...*

978 1 84616 230 5

Rorie and Elsie's parents have
disappeared. Just like that. And with only
their cruel uncle to look after them, the girls
are swept off to his miserable boarding
school. But the sisters are determined to
escape their uncle's grip – and discover the
truth behind their parents' disappearance...

*Dressing up has never been
such an adventure...*

978 1 84616 231 2

Rorie and Elsie are living the high life with
the queen of fashion, Nolita Newbuck...but
the search for their missing parents
continues. When Rorie unearths some of
Nolita's secrets, the sisters have to go on the
run once again. But what can they do when
nothing and nobody are what they seem?

Dressing up has never been such an adventure...

fiona dunbar

The Silk Sisters

tiger-lily GOLD

978 1 84616 232 9

Rorie and Elsie's parents are missing, and time is running out. The mission to rescue them will take the girls on a dangerous journey, deep into the nerve centre of the corporate machine that is robbing people of their identities. Can the Silk sisters reach their mum and dad before it's too late?

...o *by Fiona Dunbar...*

ISBN 978 1 84616 238 1 £5.99

Pablo has a gift – a secret gift

When Pablo discovers he can predict the future through
the cartoons he draws, he can hardly believe his luck. But
what seems to be a brilliant discovery soon turns into a
terrible burden, as Pablo's secret is discovered by the
wrong kind of people. Kidnapped and in a foreign
country, with only a cartoon for company – will Pablo
be able to use his gift to escape?

*Expect the unexpected in this
off-the-wall adventure!*

"Fresh, funny and captivating." *The Times*